1 MONTH OF
FREE
READING

at

www.ForgottenBooks.com

By purchasing this book you are eligible for one month membership to ForgottenBooks.com, giving you unlimited access to our entire collection of over 700,000 titles via our web site and mobile apps.

To claim your free month visit:
www.forgottenbooks.com/free775252

ISBN 978-0-483-60011-9
PIBN 10775252

CONSTANCE.

A NOVEL.

In a word, my work is digressive, and it is progressive
too, and at the same time.—STERNE.

IN THREE VOLUMES.

VOL. I.

LONDON:

RICHARD BENTLEY, NEW BURLINGTON STREET.

(SUCCESSOR TO H. COLBURN.)

1833.

LONDON :

IBOTSON AND PALMER, PRINTERS, SAVOY STREET, STRAND.

ADVERTISEMENT.

It has been justly remarked, that if persons of observation and experience, were merely to relate what they individually see and hear, in the course of even a moderately long life ; and if they were to enter into the particulars of their recollections with the same minuteness, that they would employ in detailing them for the amusement of a friend in a fireside conversation, such communications would be far more amusing, perhaps more remarkable, than many novels. How much, even in the most careless discourse, is often afforded for subject of serious reflection, and of painful interest ! Casual remarks in a stage-coach, narratives mutilated, and enfeebled, by being transmitted even to the third hand; or, what is worse, the history of deep woes, or the description of comic scenes, distorted and coloured by a tasteless lover of the marvellous; all present to the thinking mind, matter for serious speculation.

To make these available in a work, combining fact with fiction, has been the aim of the Author of these volumes; endeavouring, at the same time, to avoid introducing all incidents but such as are strictly probable; and aiming to inculcate that species of moral lesson, which a natural picture of the affairs of life, its passions, its interests, and its calamities, must inevitably convey.

CONSTANCE.

CHAPTER I.

" Sir, he hath never fed on the dainties that are bred in
a book,
He hath not eat paper, as it were; he hath not drunk
ink,
His intellect is not replenished."

SHAKSPEARE.

" THOMAS," said the precise Mrs. Cattell, an
elderly matron, resident at the borough of
Newberry, to her servant, as he brought in the
high-necked silver tea-urn, " this water don't
boil, Thomas."

The words conveyed no very important
meaning, but they were uttered in a tone so
different to the apathetic manner habitual to

...s Catull, that her unconsequential domestic, murmured, as servants were want to be, fifty years ago, did condescend, as he was quitting ... to turn round and look at her.—"She ...in a fuss—a miff about something," was ...internal ejaculation, while his audible ...speculation consisted of this laconic reply, "This here water do boil, ma'am."

"You're quite in a taking, Martha," observed Mr. Catull, who now came forward ...scene of action, from a high-backed ...which in summer he was want to pla... I could look out up... the Church ...ter, to encounter ...p... of the Spect... ...rough paper by... ...ster by his side ...that period of ...

"Thomas w... ...n dear; he's ... ...bothered wit...

"Bless me... ...here year?"

"And if...

Thomas well knew that those words ⟨obscured⟩ brought his mistress to reason; and ⟨setting⟩ down the toast at the same time, he ⟨retired⟩, having said, as he thought, just enough.

Mrs. Cattell looked aghast, and poured out the tea, tranquillized as if by a charm. To all appearance the old people might have been comfortable, for around them were all the attributes of peace, and the usual accompaniments of prosperity. They sat in a kind of summer parlour, one window of which, by ⟨...⟩ a very unusual indulgence, was allowed to remain open about three or four inches, so that the fragrance of the jasmine without was fully perceptible, whilst one or two of its ⟨sister⟩ sprays were even bold enough to intrude their starry blossoms within the room. The ⟨prospect⟩ ⟨with⟩out comprized no greater extent than a ⟨small⟩ garden; but all prospects were much ⟨the s⟩ame to Mr. and Mrs. Cattell. Within ⟨the roo⟩m, a neatly arranged tea equipage, on a ⟨Pe⟩mbroke table, bespoke the approach of ⟨that soc⟩ial meal, before the arrival of ⟨such⟩ ⟨hours⟩ of the day are usually at an end; ⟨and thr⟩ough the streams of vapour ⟨which⟩

Mrs. Cattell, that her consequential domestic, humoured, as servants were wont to be, fifty years ago, did condescend, as he was quitting the room, to turn round and look at her. " She is in a fuss—a miff about something," was Thomas's internal ejaculation, while his audible expostulation consisted of this laconic reply, " This here water *do* boil, ma'am."

" You're quite in a taking, Martha," observed Mr. Cattell, who now came forward into the scene of action, from a high-backed chair, which in summer he was wont to place where he could look out upon the Church clock; in winter, to ensconce by the fire-side; whilst a volume of the Spectator, which he was reading through, paper by paper, was placed on a dumb waiter by his side, to accelerate his slumbers at either period of the year.

" Thomas won't stand it long, I can tell you, my dear; he's not a man to be run after, nor interfered with."

" Bless me, Mr. Cattell, he's stood it these fifteen year."

" And if I don't give you satisfaction,— ma'am——" said Thomas, re-entering the room.

Thomas well knew that those words always brought his mistress to reason; and setting down the toast at the same time, he retreated, having said, as he thought, just enough.

Mrs. Cattell looked aghast, and poured out the tea, tranquillized as if by a charm. To all appearance the old people might have been comfortable, for around them were all the attributes of peace, and the usual accompaniments of prosperity. They sat in a kind of summer parlour, one window of which, by way of a very unusual indulgence, was allowed to remain open about three or four inches, so that the fragrance of the jasmine without was richly perceptible, whilst one or two of its slender sprays were even bold enough to intrude their starry blossoms within the room. The prospect without comprized no greater extent than a flower garden; but all prospects were much the same to Mr. and Mrs. Cattell. Within the room, a neatly arranged tea equipage, on a little Pembroke table, bespoke the approach of that social meal, before the arrival of which the cares of the day are usually at an end; whilst through the streams of vapour which issued from the bubbling and hissing urn, the declining rays of the summer sun were playing, gilding the white papered walls of the apartment with prismatic hues.

On Mrs. Cattell's brow there sat, however, indications of suppressed discontent. She looked as if she had all the troubles of Christendom working within her small compass of mind.

" Thomas won't be here long, nor Mitten neither, if your ward is to turn the house upside down, Mr. Cattell. Mitten won't like to be bringing her up warm water half-a-dozen times a-day, Mr. Cattell; and as to the getting up of her fine linen ——"

Here the entrance of Thomas again pacified the good lady; her voice dropped, and she looked as meek as a lamb. But his controlling presence withdrawn, her complaints broke forth again.

" It was very unkind of Colonel Courtenay to die, and leave you charge of his daughters."

" That is to say, very unkind of him to trouble us with his daughters, for dying he could not help, Mrs. Cattell, as I conceit," replied Mr. Cattell, as if he were just speaking the plain truth, and nothing more.

" True, Mr. Cattell; but what have I to do with young ladies? They are so bred up, now-a-days, as to be of no use but to play on spinets, and to hem flounces. I don't suppose now, Miss Courtenay could lend a hand to preserves, and would choose weigh out the sugar."

" Better not trust her, better not trust her, Mrs. Cattell."

" I don't intend, Mr. Cattell; but I know all my servants will give me warning. Dubster don't like young ladies; Mitten don't like young ladies; Thomas can't abear them; Sarah's fond of children, but a young lady's another thing."

" Not more trouble than a lap-dog," rejoined Mr. Cattell, not at all meaning to say a humorous thing, and casting an eye at a pert, shaggy-eared favourite, who stood up on his hinder legs, begging for a piece of cake, looking as if he was listening to the argument, and ready to take a part with the first person that offered him a sufficient bribe.

" There, Vicky, be quiet," said Mrs. Cattell peevishly.

" They've got now to that pass, to wear no pockets," she resumed thoughtfully.

" Who, the dogs, my dear ?"

" Fye, Mr. Cattell! there's Mrs. De Courcy carries her pocket kerchief in her hand—it's quite indecent. There's Miss Pearson ——"

" Well, well, Mrs. Cattell, I am not going to take charge of Mrs. De Courcy, nor Miss Pearson neither ; Miss Courtenay's Miss Courtenay — she must conform to regular hours."

" She must, Mr. Cattell,"

" Attend the card assembly regular."

" She should, Mr. Cattell."

" Then, Martha, what more can you wish for? She a'n't a bull-dog, nor a hyæna, that you should be so afraid of her. I would not put her in the best room neither. As I wrote to her," he continued, pulling out a venerable letter-case, and taking out the copy of a letter—" We breakfast at a quarter before eight for eight precisely."

" Good, Mr. Cattell."

" And we expect you are not to be sitting up late of a night"—he continued reading. " Mrs. Cattell don't like candles alight late of a night."

" Thank you, Mr. Cattell—neither I do," said Mrs. Cattell.

" So then, I think, my dear, you need not be downcast; you fidget yourself too much, Mrs. Cattell, as I conceit," added the old gentleman, folding up his precious composition, and putting it into his pocket-book.

" She isn't so bad as a young man, Mrs. Cattell," he resumed, in a consolatory tone. " What think you of a boy for a ward, Mrs. Cattell ?"

" A boy, Mr. Cattell! I should be dead in a week. A boy! I couldn't stay in the house with one a day; and as for Thomas, Mitten, Dubster, Sarah—they would think the world was come to an end if such a thing as a boy was to be thrust upon us! No," she pursued, as if relieved from the dread of a heavy misfortune, " that would be a judgment upon us; a boy indeed, wearing the shoes off his feet,

without even wiping them at the door : we are
not so badly off as that, neither."

Mr. Cattell, despite his reluctance and that
of his wife to the responsibility of his young
charge, was reputed in Newberry to be the
most suitable man in the world for such an
office; for he was beyond the middle age of
life, sedate, of creditable descent, the most un-
tainted respectability, and of habits unquestion-
ably sober, decent, and regular. Mrs. Cattell
was equally unexceptionable. Not a breath of
scandal had ever blown near the fair fabric of
her virtues. Her demeanour was exemplary,
from her deportment every Sunday at church,
where she sat bolt upright with a large green
fan before her face, to her nightly dealing and
shuffling at cards, which were thought inimi-
table. As she had no family, the voice of
censure could not be directed to her through
that channel, by means of which the most
virtuous parents are often blamed; for though
it be a great pleasure to criticize one's neighbours, it is a far greater pleasure to censure
their children. To crown the whole, as in a

funeral sermon, Mrs. Cattell was reputed most orderly and industrious. A large lion (in worsted-work only) lay before her parlour fire; this was the labour of her earlier years; but a cat, with floss silk whiskers, had, in an urn rug, been the purpose of her life during the more important period of her middle age; to say nothing of a lady, a lamb, and a peacock, embroidered in fine silk, and only un-covered upon certain occasions. Latterly, since her eyes had become indifferent, she had con-fined herself to knitting bed-quilts, and the manufacture of tape trimming, in which latter art she had acquired a degree of fame by no means ephemeral. The three Miss Seagraves' best dresses were garnished with it, and there was scarcely a lady in Newberry who had not a collar, or an apron, or a habit-shirt, or some piece of dress into which it was not introduced. To describe Mrs. Cattell's mind or heart, after this dissertation, were fruitless. No one ever thought about those. Such articles were not necessary in her routine of existence; they might even have been troublesome. It was of no consequence what hers were, since she never troubled herself about either heart or mind in other people.

As to Mr. Cattell, he was just such another piece of human machinery as his wife. For years he had not varied five minutes in any customary avocation of the day. Next to his wife, he seemed to value his watch most of any of his appurtenances, not that he was deficient in a due regard for any one of his possessions. His virtues and his history were just what would figure well upon a tombstone. He was a faithful husband, an indulgent master, an upright magistrate, a liberal donor (once a year) to the poor. He died in a ripe old age, and left not a numerous progeny to create any confusion, by the insertion of a number of unsightly names beneath his own. His name still shines in gold letters upon a large black board in Newberry church, as having bequeathed five pounds yearly to be divided among twelve old women. In short, he was a most exemplary man ; he only wanted feeling and sense, but he performed his part in life very well without either qualification.

The other individual concerned in the conversation which has been related, was the orphan daughter of an officer, who, as well as his wife, had died early. Miss Courtenay, and a younger sister, had been committed to the charge of Mr. Cattell for the period of their minority, until the seventeenth year of which they had been recommended to remain at school.

The elder of these young orphans had alone even a faint recollection of having ever been dear to any one, except her sister. They had been cast upon society, and were expected to give no trouble, and to be irreproachable in conduct, at an age when other children have their failings regarded with indulgence, and their good impulses magnified by parental fondness. Constance and Emily had known sufficiently what it was to benefit by presiding care, but had never felt the charm of voluntary affection. Yet, in the elder sister, the deprivation of domestic ties had not been attended by indifference to what her young mind pictured of them. She had often longed to share the over fond caresses which she saw lavished upon her schoolfellows—to know that there was some one longing for the holidays on her account—to

try what it was to be spoiled. Her affections,
naturally ardent, running however in one current, had become the more genuine. She knew
but one living being that belonged to her, and
that was her sister. Emily, it is true, was but
a child, but that circumstance rendered their
sisterly affection less liable to those

> Cataracts and breaks,
> Which humour interposed, too often makes.

The little varieties of thumping, pinching,
and scratching, which seldom however diminish
love, even for a time, in young children, were
totally undreamed of, between two girls in
whose ages there was four years difference.
Obliged, however, not only to depend upon
herself, but to feel that another being was
mainly dependant upon her, the naturally
buoyant spirits of the elder of the sisters had
been early kept in restraint by that consideration; not that her disposition at this period
of her life displayed anything of a chastened or
melancholy temperament, for her bereavements
had taken place too early in her career to occasion, upon recollection, more than a moment's

seriousness: a wish, perhaps, that she had a
home of her own, a mother who was obliged to
love her, and who would caress her, as she
never was caressed by any human being—for
whose endearments are like those of a mother's?
But the thought was soon dissipated, and the
very absence of those endearments gave a
cheerful independence to the character, for
which the idolized object of parental affection
might sometimes advantageously exchange the
consciousness of being fondly, and perhaps
foolishly, beloved.

Formed under these circumstances, the character of Constance, at sixteen years of age,
might seem to differ little from that of most
girls of the same situation in life. Carefully
and judiciously instructed, those frivolities
which engross so large a portion of female
attention and ingenuity, when the vanity of
mothers is interested in display, had been wisely
disregarded in the system steadily and unre-
lentingly pursued in her behalf. No fashionable
nor fond relative had interfered to urge the necessity of her annoying her associates with bad
music, or with the jargon of criticism upon

current literature. Her natural tastes had, however, directed her to cultivate accomplishments; and the habit of applying to all things with energy, had enabled her to pursue them with success. To literary avocations she had retired, as to indulgences which were considered as interruptions to the routine of her daily occupations. The charms of poetry were neither, in her case, depreciated by a painful and precise committal to memory; nor the solid excellencies of English and Foreign writers rendered vapid by premature familiarity, before the mind could comprehend their beauties. What she read, she read with enthusiasm; and it was her lot, in various passages of her after-life, to acknowledge, almost as the chief boon of Providence granted to her, the power of abstraction,—of being able to divest her mind of all other impressions, and of entering exclusively into the subject placed before her. So far was she indebted to art; but nature had even done more. Sensibility, moderated by a native integrity of character, which led her to form just notions of the limits to which she was authorized to allow feeling to impel her, was the predominant attribute of

one, who, in her journey through life, fully
experienced the necessity of feeling rightly, as
a preparation to the desirable end of thinking
rightly. Such a process is indispensable in the
formation of a moral character. It is useless
to talk of principles as within our compass, if
the heart be not disposed to admit the virtuous
emotions, of which those principles are not the
basis, but the result.

About the time when Constance reached
womanhood, greater attention, perhaps, even
than in the present day, was allotted to female
education. Emancipated from the levelling
decree, which ranked them merely as household drudges, women, during the latter years
of the eighteenth century, more especially
among the middling ranks, ran into the opposite extreme of over cultivation. It may be
considered doubtful whether such is not, even
now, the case; at least in so far as relates to
the multiplicity of objects proposed for female
ambition to achieve. But this is a digression
—and it is merely intended as a preface to the
remark, that such was not the misfortune of
Constance. She was neither crammed with

literature herself, nor did she attempt to suffo-
cate plain-sailing people with hard words, nor
to exhaust the weary with a volume of instructive talk in the high key, like the little heroes
and heroines of good books. In fact, very young
ladies cannot be said to have any conversation.
Experience, knowledge of society, acquirements
gradually and imperceptibly accumulated, are
requisite before a person can be properly said
to converse. Our heroine, at seventeen, was a
creature rather to look at than to listen to. A
deep consciousness of her own limited resources,
and a trembling sensibility to rebuffs, rendered
her silent among strangers; nor would any, but
the discerning eye, have descried, amidst the
simplicity of youth, the dawnings of a mind
superior to that of most women—equal, perhaps, to many masculine understandings.

The female character is, from its attributes,
peculiarly under the controul of circumstances,
and the influence of other, and of stronger
natures. There cannot be a more momentous
condition than that of a young woman under
twenty. A fool may win her admiration, and
her character becomes for a time, at least, fri-

volous. Many a noble spirit in woman has been checked by an ill-placed, first affection ; but if she be fortunate enough to place an early dependence upon a worthy object, the tenor of her life is determined.

It is observable, that in youth women cannot understand friendship towards men. Girls never stop at that point. There is always a tinge of love in their sentiments towards intimate associates in the other sex. Hence the dangerous ascendancy acquired by their male instructors, and by other less attractive and less meritorious individuals, over women who have been even delicately nurtured.

But Constance had never felt this latent sentiment in the faintest degree aroused, when she reached the house of her guardian, there first to enter life on her own responsibility. She had seen, indeed, some society in the metropolis, where the connexions of her deceased parents had afforded her opportunities of sight-seeing and of party-going; but she had beheld the surface of society only. Her exterior consequently had been affected by her partial introduction into the gay world, but her mind had neither been improved, nor her heart affected by it. It was only her outward deportment which had been changed by it, and in that she was both graceful and distinguished. Nor could these advantages of mind and person continue, without having their effect upon her destiny; and indeed she was destined to experience, in no ordinary degree, the harshness of those penalties which women pay for superiority, either personal or mental.

CHAPTER II.

Charles. Well, George, what of the place?

George. Place! good!—here the word town would be misplaced. The houses, in one long straggling street, appear as if they had been shut up for an age, and only taken out for airing; the flags bear the chisel of a century, untrodden; our ostler seems as immovable as the horse-shoe nailed upon the gate-post: but, like other far-off regions, it has its divinities. I have seen——

The Assize, M.S. Comedy.

A TALL house in a street, accessible by a regular flight of stone steps, and dignified by the interposition of a small space of garden; on the left, a long row of gable-ended and red-brick tenements; on the right, an ancient gate-way; to the front, the demure aspect of a Quaker's substantial dwelling, neat, regular, and in perfect repair; and backed by a small open space, in ancient days the butts or archery ground of the borough—Such was the house which received Constance upon her removal from school.

At her age, girls are tolerably independent of what is called comfort, and their ideas on that score are easily reconcileable with habit. I well remember, however, the chilling aspect of the abode which destiny had assigned to Constance. The painful neatness, and melancholy order which prevailed there—attributes in themselves delightful when combined with cheerfulness, and enlivened by warmth, but mournful, when they are symptoms of excessive precision, extreme retirement, or absence of occupation. The unimpaired matting at the door, the carpet, seemly both from sedulous care and from little use—the old-fashioned, untempting settee, framed, as it might appear, for backs either without joints, or in a state of petrifaction — the covered fire-screens — and, above all, the locked-up book-case,—bespeak a sphere admirably adapted for automatons, but ill-suited to thinking, moving, breathing, eating and drinking human beings. That the inhabitants of her guardian's abode were living, sentient creatures, was apparent to Constance; but that they were thinking beings, constituted in the same manner as the companions she had left behind her, was a fact of which, for some time, it was not easy for her to feel certain. For several days, indeed, after her arrival, she took little pains to study the characters of those with whom many years of her life would probably be spent. Somewhat timid, and from the desolateness of her early years little accustomed to look for fondness from those whom she might naturally expect to regard her as a trouble, Constance, for the first week of her arrival, passed much time in the garden of her guardian. This garden, afterwards one of the minor blessings of her life, was dedicated to the genius of regularity, as much as the house was under the influence of that deity. But if this presiding genius had her full sway in the formation and care of this spot, nature, and a warm summer, had, at the time of Constance's first entrance, in some degree defeated her intentions.

I have sometimes thought that the chronology of flowers would form as curious a subject

as the fashion of our costumes, so diligently
portrayed by antiquaries. The gay gum Cistus,
the voluptuous Stock, the brilliant Larkspur,
luxuriant Convolvolus, and unrivalled Provence
rose, have long since yielded to the Ixias, Lo-
bilias, Bigonias, Bignonias, and other numerous tribes of exotics, now chiefly in vogue;
but the guardians of our heroine would have
expired with astonishment, had they been told
that Geraniums were varied by seeds, or Hy-
drangias changed in hue by a simple process.
Their plants, like themselves, had bloomed,
year after year, on their native soil. Selec-
tion and arrangement were points wholly disregarded in their horticulture. To produce one
universal luxuriant sheet of blossom—to mingle
all hues and all families together as custom or
accident decided—to extirpate weeds, and to
avoid every indication of taste, seemed to be
all their care. Hence were the borders of the
long and undeviating gravel-walk of Mr. Cattell's garden, fringed with a natural garniture
of shrubs and annuals, so luxuriantly gaudy
and varied, that the beholder almost sickened
with the first impressions of one of our most

irradicable pleasures—the love of flowers. Pluck
where you would, you seemed to diminish not—
trample where you would, you were surrounded
by a forest of rival beauties—too much disbo-
noured by any comparison even with the fairest of
the human race. But this pleasurable, though
ignoble scene, was graced by the proximity of an
object to which Constance, first from devotional,
and afterwards from tenderer associations, often
reverted with reverential gaze. This was no less
a feature in the borough than the Parish church,
an antiquated pile, built after the fashion of
the middle ages and midland counties, with
delicately pointed pinnacles, each surmounted
by a vane. The house of God is ever a heart-
gladdening object in a landscape—a point upon
which the eye, directed by the affections, is
certain to rest. Wretched is the man whose
thoughts are so surrendered to this world, that
he can hurry by an ancient, holy edifice, without one momentary abstraction from his pursuits ! Yet, I believe—and scandalous it is to
say it—that the good people of Newberry regarded St. Michael's tower with more compla-
cency that its chimes, at six, summoned them

to their sessional meetings, their whist and commerce tables; and that the same deep and swinging peel warned them, by a lucky arrangement of our ancestors, to depart at nine, to a yet more complete cessation from the workings of intellect, than they had enjoyed all day in their arm-chairs.

Constance, of course, attended morning and afternoon service on the first Sunday after her arrival at Newberry. She blamed herself for almost looking forward to it as piece of gaiety, so tranquil had been the tenor of her week's initiation into the pleasures of independence. She thought herself somewhat childish for the anxiety which she felt in fitting on the London bonnet which she had brought—the fears that the white rose on the one side might be thought too low—the bow in the other direction too conspicuous. Yet she need not have been apprehensive, for attired with a neatness, simplicity, and moderation, to which country ladies were then strangers, she appeared, in the streets of Newberry, as a being the like of which had never been seen there before. At length the well-known chime was heard to peal; at the commencement of the first bell, Mr. Cattell changed his coat and shoes; and Mrs. Cattell appeared on the stairs with a high-topped, close-poke, grey silk bonnet, decorated with black lace. When the second monitor roused the irreligious and slumbering from their apathy, Mr. Cattell stuck on the three-cornered shovel hat, which fitted his wig, not his head: the respectable Thomas appeared with his huge bag; and Mrs. Cattell drew over her shoulders her black silk mantle, edged with curious lace, and confined to her slender waist with great precision. At length they all crept out, our blooming heroine looking as little in harmony with her companions, as a modern picture would appear by the side of an old-fashioned portrait.

It was the arrangement of the Cattell family to enter their highly-boasted parlour pew, adjacent to the chancel, just as the introductory hymn struck up. On this occasion they were, however, a little sooner, and Constance had an opportunity, without dereliction from her sacred duties, of observing the clergyman, as he passed down the long aisle to the reading-desk. She was much pleased with his appearance, and was impressed by it with the sentiment of the extreme beauty of early piety, and with the interest attached to youth combined with holiness. His regular, and somewhat aquiline features, expressed benevolence, tinctured, but not checked, by seriousness;—his dark and clustering hair curled on a finely-formed and placid brow—his figure was slight, but easy, and was dignified by the folds of his sacred vestment. But when he began that monitory address, which is at once solemn, persuasive, and comprehensive, Constance thought that she could have drunk in every sound of tones so full, expressive, and melodious. Whilst she fervently accompanied him with her heart through the service, the sudden entrance of a person into Mr. Cattell's pew diverted her attention. She started, for, to her, the young gentleman who now took his seat opposite to her, appeared as if he might have figured in the gay circles of the metropolis on the same sabbath, and not have been deemed unfashionable. He was about the middle size, but of a figure admirably proportioned. His features were enlivened by so much, and such varied expression, and his dark blue eyes were so replete with intelligence, that one could not call him plain. Yet it was an air of high breeding and of perfect elegance about him that pleased, rather than positive good looks. His dress, though carefully studied, on him looked easy, and although his address was confident, yet there was no degree of insolent assurance in his manner. Constance at her first glance guessed him to be about five-and-twenty; had she given a second, younger. She concluded that he was a stranger, with a seat. A low, and well-trained curtsey on remonious bow between the two gentlemen showed her, nevertheless, that there was some acquaintance. Somewhat conscious of a little undue curiosity, however, she inquired not his name, but heard her guardian muttering to his wife, " that perhaps Sir Charles's own pew would be ready for him next Sunday." To this the reply was:—" My dear, I shall not go this afternoon, and Sir Charles Marchmont never goes twice, therefore if you wish to accommodate the Evans's, you may." A mystified sort of mumbling from Mr. Cattell, followed by special directions to Thomas to order his " grey hackney at three," seemed an evasion to this proposal, and left the important matter dubious.

When the bells tolled for evening service, Constance, whose romantic as well as devotional feelings had been excited by a visit to the interior of St. Michael's, requested, and obtained permission, to go again to church. She was now chaperoned by the venerable Mistress Susan Mitten, Mrs. Cattell's other soul, who reigned over the destinies of the nether regions in her master's mansion.

Whilst Constance walked to church, followed, rather than accompanied by her duenna, she felt some disposition to inquire the name and circumstances of the young intruder into her guardian's pew, whom she had seen in the morning; but a sense of what was due to the sacred edifice, and to that unity of idea which ought to prevail therein, restrained her. She congratulated herself that he would not again present himself, but in this expectation she was deceived: he was there when she arrived.

It is difficult to conceive a mode of religious worship more simple, impressive, and even solemn, than the evening service of our church, performed whilst the shades of night are gathering around us. The autumnal day was fast drawing to a close; the high Gothic windows admitted a softened light upon the small and scattered congregation—the select few of a lukewarm parish— who were dispersed among the "long-drawn aisles." The old, the poor, and the afflicted, were there; but the young and happy were wending their gladsome way along the fair meadows by the river side. Constance was one of the few in life's early promise, who found it pleasant to repair to the courts of her God. On this occasion it might almost seem that the sermon was peculiarly adapted to her situation. The young, and earnest preacher spoke of the helplessness, and expatiated upon the duties, of the orphan state. He described the sorrowing parent, bequeathing the charge of his infant race to that God who called them into being. He represented our heavenly Father as the peculiar guardian òf the destitute, and exhorted the bereaved and the faint-hearted to throw all their care upon him. Constance took these admonitions deeply to heart. A sense of her condition pressed upon her, for the first time, heavily, and almost prophetically; she felt that she had now entered upon life, destitute of most of those ties which could endear it; and a vague consciousness of danger, an indefinite fear of injury and of temptation, made her spirit sink within her.

" O !" exclaimed she within herself, " had I but a friend—a monitor like him who has thus called forth these apprehensions, how would I cherish and pursue his counsels !" Serious, even to dejection, she returned home, nor saw, what all the ladies of Newberry would have died rather than have missed seeing, the gay young Baronet escorting the widow, Mrs. De Courcy, home across the market-place.

CHAPTER III.

And lo ! the crowded ball-room is alive
With restless motion, and a humming noise
Like on a warm spring-morn a sunny hive.

WILSON.

SOON after the arrival of Constance at Newberry, she was invited to a ball, given by a
neighbouring family, as a sort of annual enter-
tainment. Our readers must not suppose that
it was any thing of a very splendid nature,
especially as the chances of beaux were in those
parts few, and dependent on many contin-
gencies, and the presence of musicians by no
means certain. The society of Newberry, at
this period, differed, in no respect, from that
of most country towns, forty or fifty years
ago, saving, that it was more genteel, or, in
other terms, more contracted, than in some

other places of the same extent. The younger branches of aristocratic families, elderly clergymen, retired officers, and physicians without practice, of whom its inhabitants were partly composed, looked with contempt upon the commercial portion of their fellow-townsmen, who had, however, the superiority in wealth, and perhaps in intelligence, over their haughty neighbours. Hence, the vulgarity of the commercialists remained unchanged by admission into the more refined circles of their self-exalted, but detested superiors ; whilst the ignorance, narrow-mindedness, pride, and self-delusion of the latter, were undiluted by any deviations from their own peculiar set. It happened, also, that a remarkable dearth of attraction among the aristocratic party prevailed. They had no public spirit : no taste for innovation; no desire for improvement; and were mostly of an age to prefer the card assembly to the dancing-room. There were few young persons amongst them. If you went into a party, you heard nothing but asthmatic coughs, and saw few of your company free from some infirmity. The young and blooming were as misplaced here as roses on a sepulchre. The long, long hand at whist, the unfathomable poole of quadrille, are recreations which deprive youth of its freshness, and give a calculating turn to the mind, and stiff appearance to the manners. Hence, few of those who were once young ladies in Newberry, had been so fortunate as to obtain husbands. The Newberry partics were so notoriously dull, that no agreeable young man could be prevailed to take more than one trial of them, and the air of Newberry began to be deemed a sort of antidote to love. Such was the state of things when Constance arrived there.

But, in the neighbourhood, affairs were better managed. Household establishments were more enlarged: cards had not, from nightly repetition, become indispensable; and, where there were young people, it was found necessary to have some amusements for them natural to their age. True it was, that the belles were in those regions clumsy, and the beaux rather of the Nimrod, than of the Chesterfield order. The young ladies might be vastly expert in horsemanship, archery, and gardening, but they were mightily deficient in the graces of the mind, and in the arts which throw a charm around retirement, or instil into society its chief zest. Along with these deficiencies in intellectual culture, much pride, folly, and overweening vanity, are certain to prevail; and, at the period to which I refer, they did prevail, to a much more uncommon degree than at the present time. Hence, to the refined, the reflective, and the sensitive, that solitude of the heart, which is sometimes exchanged for a far more dangerous condition, not unfrequently produced by force of contrast between one favoured individual and the less engaging objects who act as foils to that personage.

Constance received, with no slight degree of pleasure, the invitation which called her into something like social intercourse. The monotony of her life was not, indeed, displeasing to her, for she had but few and transitory scenes of pleasure with which to contrast it; nor, were there as yet aroused in her innocent bosom, those passions which render excitement necessary to preserve us from despair. Cheerful, because occupied, and often gay from mere animal spirits, the artificial wants of young ladies of the present generation were unknown to her. Nevertheless her heart glowed within her at the thoughts of a ball.

The scene of action was at a village about five miles distant from Newberry; the invitations had been numerous, and post-chaises, barouches, and even mourning coaches, were in constant requisition during the course of this eventful evening. The hair-dresser, who generally loitered at his shop-window all day, was now in urgent request; and he conferred the last touches upon the unadorned ringlets of Constance, before the chaperon appointed by Mrs. Cattell to supply her place arrived to take charge of the young lady: for it was well known in Newberry, that the good, precise Mrs. Cattell, could never keep her eyes open after ten o'clock, and that her husband, who slept the whole evening, was equally early in his hours of retirement. Constance was therefore consigned to the guidance of Miss Monckton, one of the most exemplary, aristocratic elderly virgins, that ever blossomed on the single thorn in her native town. The character of this lady deserves to be so far distinguished from the class to which she belonged, as that its harsher points were softened by benevolence, and that her fearless sincerity was in general untinctured by ill-nature. Perhaps there is no person so little, in general, to be loved, as an high-bred and poor old maid. Proud from education, morose from circumstances; frivolous from necessity, or, rather from the absence of inducements to better things; envious until a certain period of life, and when the sear and yellow leaf of age falls around her, inactive, selfish, and repining, she forms a hedge-row in society which few would be willing to approach. With Miss Monckton, however, some variation existed. Contemptuous, and even sarcastic in her manners, her conduct was often at variance with the system which the singly blessed seem frequently resolved to adopt. She was even reproached by her sister-sufferers, with the sin of liking to see " young people gay," a propensity not often apt to be gratified among the select assemblies of Newberry.

Entrenched in a lutestring dress of formidable compass, her head surmounted by one of those turbans worn in former days, from which a tail of its own material was left dangling, and which, in the main structure, appeared not unlikely soon to descend upon the nose, her grey eyes twinkling with a transitory excitement, and every muscle of her worn-out countenance in play, Miss Monckton surveyed, with some degree of pride, the fair girl whom it was her office to introduce. Her first observation was that Miss Courtenay was like Lady Harriet Somebody, who had figured at the county and race-balls some thirty years ago. Her next remarks extended to the modesty of Miss Courtenay's attire, which she much commended ; " For upon my word," said the good lady, as she stepped into the carriage, " Mrs. Tomlinson, the other night, appeared at the Hunt ball in a white satin —*chemise*, it appeared to be ; and her three sisters, the Miss Haydons, all in chemises also : married ladies now-a-days show as much of their trowsers as their little boys do."

" But," continued she, " you must not expect to eclipse the five Miss Tribes. Among such a collection of *beauties*, you have no chance;"—and then, with a slight laugh, she pursued; " I'll lay my life they are dressed with huge red roses in their hair, all alike, boddices laced with blue, or some such trumpery."

" Are they handsome, madam?"

" My dear, they have plenty of flesh and blood, good wholesome complexions, no over sensibility there; nothing pulls them down—they can dance down forty couple without being out of breath, but no wonder with such legs. Such legs! Do you know the young gentlemen, my dear?"

" No, ma'am, I do not know any of the family; I was merely told that Tribe was the name of the lady who gives the ball to-night, and that there were several daughters."

" Several!" my dear, there's a constant fresh supply, a never-ending replenishment of the quiver. Five are introduced into society, and two twin sisters were introduced last summer into the nursery. I don't suppose one of the elder girls has had an offer yet. Charitable would be the man who would take a couple of

them off Mr Tribe's hands. And then the sons!
the pride of their poor mother, who tells you
that Tom has *face,* and James *figure.* Tom,
I should observe, is scarcely five feet high: he
has the round, healthy, unmeaning, but, as
some people think, good-looking face of the
Tribe family; but James is immoderately ugly.
Do you know what Sir Charles calls him? Sir
Charles Marchmont."

" Sir Charles Marchmont, who sits in our
pew at church?"

" Yes, my dear. The heir apparent—(not
very apparent yet, for his estates to come are
mortgaged to the Lord knows-whom)—however, the heir apparent, as they call it, to the
Priory, and other property round Newberry.
Well, this Sir Charles, who is more witty than
wise, entitles this man of figure, this Mr. James
Tribe, Asmodeus."

" Vastly satirical," thought Constance; and
no doubt this Sir Charles is, what he looks, a
supercilious man of fashion, who despises the
simplicity of these country gentry. " And
what sort of a person," she inquired, " in mind,
I mean, is Sir Charles himself?"

" O, my dear, he is a man who can do every thing, bad and good, I believe. He draws finely, dances elegantly, rides inimitably, and converses irresistibly. You know, my dear, I say what I hear. As to my own opinion of Sir Charles, I confess I think him a gentleman, as he should be, born and bred. I am told he is generous, though not rich; that he is honourable, and has, since his childhood, been a mighty favourite with old and young on his father's estate. You know his history, I suppose ?"

" I! O no !" said Constance, with some eagerness.

" His father destroyed himself, it is supposed, in a fit of jealousy of his mother, Lady Marchmont,—I know not why or wherefore. Well, this lady goes off to France or Italy, and dies there, some people say, others affirm that she is still living. Meanwhile, there is, as you know, an ancient Gothic residence, called the Priory, on the north side of the town. Lady Marchmont had a life interest in this place, therefore, until her death is ascertained, it cannot be sold, a great detriment to Sir

Charles, whose family residence, Marchmont, is shut up for want of funds to keep it up— funds which the sale of this tumbling-down old place would supply. So here he lives, part of the year in general, and amuses himself with hunting, coursing, sketching, and the like, and I am told that the young man knows how to behave himself. He has plenty of noble blood in his veins, and has been noticed in town by his high connexions on both sides. He is much attached to our Vicar, Mr. Bouverie; and I trust that the example of that excellent young man may preserve the young Baronet from the extravagance and imprudence of his mother, and the rash impulses of his father. But here we are at our journey's end. Now, my dear, be advised by me, and don't dance with *any* body."

Constance and her companion were early visitors, and, at the request of Miss Monckton, were shown into Mrs. Tribe's dressing-room, to repair such damage as might have been in-curred in their transit. Here they were diverted by the anxieties of the five Miss Tribes, whose various toilets had been completed, and who now awaited the approval of their mother in an adjacent room. At length, they descended to the drawing-room, to which they were speedily followed by our heroine and her chaperon.

Every one knows the contrivances resorted to in former days to illuminate, adorn, and enlarge a house, upon ball occasions. It has now become vulgar to stick up candles in recesses, to chalk floors, and to adorn doorways with garlands of flowers. The five Miss Tribes, in those days, thought differently. The dancing-room was like an arbour, and it would have required Aladdin's lamp to enlighten the foliage, which they had sedulously arranged on the sundry pannels and irregularities of an old-fashioned wainscot. The effect was expected to be very striking, and was certainly gratifying, as conveying to the mind of the guests the impression that great pains had been taken to do them honour, an impression always agreeable to poor human nature; but otherwise, a dread of earwigs, and a sensation of impeded air, might endanger the comfort of some fastidious belles. But all was in accordance with the taste of the times, and of the neighbourhood ; and, accordingly, the young friends of the house, and especially those who had an eye to Mr. Tom or Mr. James, applauded loudly.

The five Miss Tribes, all in yellow muslins, stood in a group, looking like a bunch of daffodils, and were pronounced—as a show of stout, healthy sisters always is—to be quite a picture; only, as Miss Monckton remarked, they had one general defect pervading the family :—they were altogether too thick—had thick ancles, thick waists, thick voices, and thick heads.

At length, the party increasing, music struck up—that sort of music which drowns the loudest voice, and makes stillness not merely a negative state of tranquillity, but an absolute pleasure. Constance was speedily entrapped into the toils of Mr. Thomas Tribe, a large-headed youth, whose upper part seemed destined for a tall and portly man, but whose nether proportions appeared not to have kept pace with the intentions of nature. He tried, however, to dance genteelly, and to converse agreeably ; and there was a happy look of perfect self-

satisfaction about him that made Constance, in
spite of some inclination to laugh at him, sym-
pathize in his good spirits. She was next consigned to the irresistible James, reputed by his
sisters to be " a marvellous fine figure," on account of his having attained to a stature some
six inches higher than his brother; but to reconcile Tom to his inferiority in this respect, the
fates had decreed that James should display
a grotesque contrariety of feature, which was
not relieved by any particular expression. He
had, however, the family self-complacency, and
was observed always to attach himself to the
prettiest woman in the room, with a perfect
insensibility to rebuffs, and a happy deficiency
in the art of discovering certain feminine stra-
tagems which were often made to elude him as
a partner. With him Constance was dancing,
when Sir Charles Marchmont and Mr. Bouverie
entered the room. She instantly met the
glances of the former, and saw that they passed
from her to her partner, with an expression
which good-breeding and good-humour alone
prevented from being very satirical. With the
bashfulness of a girl newly introduced to so-

ciety, she fancied, however, that she was in part the object of Sir Charles's sarcasm, and, with the warmth natural to her age, she took almost an instantaneous dislike to him ; yet it was curious, nor could she, in after life, account for the circumstance, that whenever she encountered him, in the dance, or passed him in the promenade, a sudden blush, and slight palpitation of the heart, gently agitated her frame.

Meanwhile, she was really anxious to become acquainted with Mr. Bouverie, but he declined all solicitations to dance, notwithstanding the five different assaults upon his vanity made by the Miss Tribes, and sundry floating observations upon the scarcity of beaux, and the predominance of the fair sex. He refused, however, their requests, not upon the plea of his clerical functions—a species of company heroism to which he was superior—but pleaded want of practice, and of dancing-shoes, and a total inability to comprehend the elaborate figures of Money Musk, the College Hornpipe, and the Boulanger, then in vogue. Unhappy man !

Had he lived in these more easy times, he might have gallopaded without knowing either tune, time, or figure; or he might soon have been initiated into the eternal first set of quadrilles; or he might, by dint of a vigorous partner, have been waltzed round in the tenacious grasp of some young lady. However, he chose to sit still, and Constance was obliged to hear a succession of regrets from most of the young ladies around her, many of whom would gladly have instructed the young and handsome Vicar, even in the difficulties of Sir Roger de Coverley, that test of memory and patience.

Shortly afterwards, however, Constance was waited upon by a deputation of Mr. Thomas, and one of his sisters, to inform her that Sir Charles wished to be introduced to her, a ceremonial to be followed, of course, by a solicitation to dance. Now Constance had enough of the woman to be somewhat perverse, so that this compliment, far from conciliating her, rather brought to a head a certain pettish spleen against Sir Charles Marchmont. To the surprise of every one about her, therefore, she declined dancing, and rejected the offer of being led off by this prime beau of the room.

" What! my dear," said Miss Monckton, " do I hear right? It is quite unaccount-able."

" Not at all, dear Miss Monckton," replied Constance;. " I do not wish to dance with any gentleman who looks down upon the company he is in."

" Looks down! And has he not a right to look down? Pray whom do you wish to put upon a par with him? Perhaps the gentleman with long bows of black galloon at his knees— Mr. Kendall, of ——, the son of a ribbon weaver? Or perhaps you think that young man preferable—Mr. Harvey, of the —— militia. Let me tell you, that his father's fa-ther was only steward to Mr. Boswell, of Boswell Court; and besides it is well-known that this Mr. Harvey, whom you perhaps ad-mire, hung himself up with a skipping-rope of his sister's when he was eighteen, for love of his mother's maid, and was only just cut down in time."

" O, my dear Miss Monckton, do take care what you say, and indeed you need not be afraid of my falling in love with Mr. Harvey— but see—do look at the partner whom Sir Charles has chosen."

The young Baronet was now leading to the dance the most notoriously plain, old young lady in Newberry. This was a Miss Pearson, one of two sisters, who had hung on hand many years after the bloom of youth had passed away. They were well-principled and well-educated women, but were also, what is inexcusable in good people, because it disparages virtue, dull, to a degree unimaginable by any, but those unhappy persons—their intimate friends. Miss Arabella Pearson was a notorious proser: she could tell you to a minute when every stage-coach passed by her door, and when it would re-pass. Her information on higher subjects was chronologically just to a second; her geographical and historical accuracy were unimpeached; but there wanted that indescribable something, that tact, or inspiration, called talent, without which a learned female is not near so good a companion as a dictionary, and a very small degree of which contributes to gild moderate acquisitions with some portion of intellectual interest. It was surmised by several of the guests at Mr. Tribe's ball, that Sir Charles selected this respectable, but ungainly lady, as a partner, chiefly to mortify the fair nymph who had previously rejected him, by showing her what he might wish her to suppose he considered as a fit successor to the scornful beauty ; just as a widower, who has lost an attractive wife, is thought to dishonour her memory by supplying her place with an illiterate, or unseemly helpmate. The affront, if intended to be such, was, however, impervious to the simple perceptions of Constance, whose attention was entirely rivetted on the extreme elegance of the young Baronet's dancing. Whilst other gentlemen sprang, kicked, crossed legs, advanced, and retired, with inexplicable steps, in which no legitimate arrangement could be discovered ; whilst some with elaborate neatness of execution, lost by precision the graces which they might be thought to have gained in study ; whilst many loitered or lounged, and seemed in the condition of

men unwillingly dragged about by their partners, and whilst others, chiefly the stout, robust
men, who wished to be accounted light figures,
spun round like tetotums ; Sir Charles, in a
style animated, yet gentle, cultivated, yet not
formal, moved through the mazes of a cotillion with an agility and elegance as far removed from the attitudes of a dancing-master, as from the awkwardness of the Tony
Lumpkins by whom he was surrounded.
Much was he doubtless to be commiserated
for the weight which he was doomed to drag
after him, in his partner ; yet he conducted
that substantial form with as much apparent
ease and address, as if her every movement
had not been out of time, and her elbows like
ton weights.

Constance, who had suffered the recent in-
fliction of poussetting with the clumsy Mr.
James Tribe, almost sighed to think that she
had relinquished such a partner as Sir Charles.
With girlish admiration she moved eagerly
towards the dance, to have a nearer inspection,
when she was way-laid by old Mr. Tribe, who
begged to introduce to her Mr. Bouverie, who,

as the officiating parish clergyman, requested
an acquaintance with his young parishioner.
Constance, with undisguised pleasure, received
this attention, and, by a strange presentiment,
regarded it even at that moment as the prelude
to an intimacy of a peculiar nature. Of love,
towards any man, she had, as yet, scarcely
even thought; but she had always cherished
the idea of some time or other discovering in
some male acquaintance, a friend on whose
counsels she could rest, and whose mind, whilst
it assimilated with her own, would yet display
powers far superior to those which she could
perceive in her ordinary female acquaintance.
Impressed with this notion, she listened to the
remarks made by Mr. Bouverie with an eagerness which quickly communicated to those
around her the notion, that she was greatly
interested in the young Vicar. He led her
into the supper-room, and was observed, in
the course of a long discussion of fowls, jel-
lies, trifles, and *jaune manges*, to present her
with a rich and clustering stock, which was, according to the fashion of old times, thrown
carelessly as a garniture of one of the dishes.

Meanwhile, notwithstanding the unfeigned, and somewhat boisterous merriment of the Tribe family, and others of a similar stamp, Sir Charles Marchmont sat abstracted in earnest conversation with Miss Monckton, who appeared to be stimulating him to some grand enterprize.

" But, my dear Miss Monckton," he was overheard to say, " it is obvious that she has taken a dislike to me. Well, I admire her discrimination in liking Bouverie, and wish him joy of the impression he has evidently made. He too is smitten : I never saw him so absorbed before. How is it possible to resist the artlessness and intelligence of that girl's smile ? Her beauty, though a quality rare enough in these parts, might be passed over, though I confess I am not the person to despise a lovely face, and, with expression——"

" Well, well, what then prevents you from being introduced to her ?"

" Not this time, my dear Miss Monckton; besides I will not interfere with Bouverie's happiness. Recommend him to her by all means ; but if you find he has no chance, then

put in, dear charitable soul, a word for me.
Well, adieu ; I see the petticoats are disappear-
ing —*au revoir* in the ball-room ; and do teach
your pretty charge to be a little less cynical,
and not to fancy, because a man happens to
be three degrees removed from a clodpole,
that he looks down upon the company he is in."

CHAPTER IV.

Unmuffle, ye faint stars, and thou, fair moon,
That wonst'st to love the traveller's benizon;
Stoop thy pale visage through an amber cloud,
And disinherit Chaos, that reigns here.

MASK OF COMUS.

THE party broke up in that healthy and seasona-
ble time which ensures vigour, enhances enjoyment, and preserves good complexions. The night
was dark, and the roads were drenched with rain;
and Miss Monckton and Constance, as they en-
rolled themselves in their cloaks, and stepped into
their cold chariot, almost envied a merry party
of six, who, for want of any conveyance equally
roomy, were returning to Newberry in a Mourning-Coach. Mr. Cattell's carriage formed the
first of the home procession, and, furnished
with lamps, was on the road at some distance

before the rest of the revellers. The two ladies within were earnest in talk—Constance expatiating in praise of Mr. Bouverie, and Miss Monckton putting in, according to instructions, a word for Sir Charles, when they were startled by a sudden descent of the carriage, and a splashing of water. Happily for their self-command, the two ladies were unconscious of the potency of Mr. Tribe's ale, to which, having had no personal experience on the subject, their minds never reverted. A little stream, however, crossing the road, had been swollen to some magnitude by the heavy rains which had fallen during the course of the evening: it was not of depth sufficient to have endangered the passage of a carriage, under the controul of a careful driver; but, unluckily, he to whom the lives of Miss Monckton and Constance were entrusted, being in a debateable state between drunkenness and sobriety, had verged into a ditch by the wayside, now forming, with the lesser waters, a pool of some extent. The vehicle in which the two ladies sat, was therefore threatened with a speedy overturn, if not with an entire submersion.

Plunged into this Slough of Despond, Constance, for the first time since her infancy, experienced in this unlooked-for extremity the agony of strong personal fear—that emotion which is known to break even the force of natural ties, in the vehemence of our instinct of self-preservation. She clung to her companion, as she perceived the horses taken off their feet, and the water reaching almost up to the carriage window. To her horror she found Miss Monckton cold and motionless, that lady having, upon the discovery of their danger, instantly fainted. The oaths of the postilion, the struggling of the horses, and the splashing of the water, were the only sounds which Constance heard, though she listened eagerly for the noise of coming travellers. At length, after a few minutes' breathless reflection, she leaned her slight form as far as possible through the window, and with the strong effort of despair, screamed piercingly for help. An interval of silence succeeded, in which the sickness of death seemed to come over her. But youth is fertile in expedients. With a trembling hand she opened one of the carriage lamps, and holding up one of the lights by way of a beacon, reiterated her agonized and plaintive entreaties. All around her seemed security and peace, contrasted with her own situation. The dark abyss, for such seemed to her the petty, yet dangerous waters beneath her, imparted to her, as the light she held gleamed over it, a sensation of horror which she had little notion that the fear of death could have imparted. She cast her eyes towards the postilion, (who, struggling and swearing alternately, seemed totally unable to avert, yet resolved fully to merit the doom which threatened him : almost hopeless, she still extended her arm, and at intervals reiterated her piercing cries for assistance.

At length, the sound of horses reached her ears, and immediately afterwards the exclamation, " Good God ! Is it possible ! Miss Monckton's carriage,—Miss Courtenay ! Bouverie, hold my horse—no, no ; I perceive the waters are too deep; I will ride to that door—you to this—open the carriage doors and let us each bear away a lady." Thus saying, and retaining, even in his real anxiety, address enough to direct his own course to the relief of the youngest and fairest of the distressed damsels, Sir Charles Marchmont rode boldly into the water, but not advancing so far as to the dangerous position in which the carriage stood. He was enabled, however, to open the carriage door on the side which Constance stood, she having previously, in the first impulse of joy, at his approach, dropped the light which she had held into the water. He then entreated her to hold out her arms towards him, conjuring her, for the preservation of her own life and that of her companion, to disregard all considerations but those of safety.

" But Miss Monckton," cried Constance, " how can I leave her in this situation ?"

" Never mind, there is help for her ; think only of yourself—extend your arms towards me ; I can then seize hold of you—of your dress, or any thing—forgive this necessary forwardness,—wait not, delay not, I entreat you, or I must plunge deeper into the water, and then—"

" O do not stir, whoever you are," cried the object of his care ; " I will do what you advise, for the waters are fast rushing into the carriage :

O sir, be firm, and let me not drop into this horrible place," she added, shuddering at the fear of a sudden descent into the pool below.

" Not for my existence," rejoined the young Baronet, with genuine zeal. " Now, dear lady, grasp this hand firmly, and, leaning forwards, I can soon rescue you from your peril."

Constance instantly complied with his instructions, and her agile form, scarcely emerged from girlhood, was speedily snatched from its post of danger, by the young and dexterous knight errant, whom Providence had sent for her rescue. In a few seconds she was conveyed, firmly grasped in his arms, to terra firma; but such was the agitation of the moment, that, had she been asked exactly how she arrived there, she would have found any reply impossible.

Meanwhile, Mr. Bouverie had a more difficult, as well as a less interesting task. It is true, that the water was far less deep on that side of the carriage where Miss Monckton sat, than on the opposite one from which Constance had recently been emancipated. But the elder lady had but recovered from her state of syncope, to an

hysterical seizure, a lady's privilege on such occasions, but extremely inconvenient and unfa-
vourable to any plans for assistance in danger.
Mr. Bouverie, who was able to ride up to the
carriage door, had first to convince her that he
was there; then, to satisfy her, that she was
not drowned; then to assure her that he could
hold her on his horse, if she would so far honour him by entrusting herself to him; then to
beg her to let him open the carriage door:
and then, there would have been the difficulty
of compassing the deliverance of a tall, gaunt
figure, inflexible in form, and opposed by scruples more foolish than delicate, in this instance,
to any very great proximity to the person of
her male deliverer. Now all this trouble and
persuasion might have been very agreeable to
Mr. Bouverie, had it been exerted in behalf of
a young, and lovely female; and probably, had
he been on the other side of the carriage, he
would have been more energetic in his entreaties. His patience, however, was beginning to
be exhausted, when he was relieved by the arrival of the Mourning Coach, filled with several
male and female denizens of Newberry, all

equally curious to know the cause of the bustle, of which they caught some glimmering, even through the shades of night. The cumbrous vehicle which arrived so opportunely, was driven securely into the midst of the swoln, but not deep, streamlet which crossed the road, and, with the assistance of Mr. Bouverie, the affrighted Miss Monckton was soon removed into its enclosure, and there, revived by the kindness, and the smelling bottles of the young and old ladies which it contained. This said coach, like a life boat, was also made available, through the means of its driver, in assisting the drunken postilion, the "head and front" of all this perturbation. By the united efforts of drunk and sober, the horses of Mr. Cattell's chariot, were, after much exertion, restored to the full use of their fore feet; and the carriage once more reinstated in its proper equilibrium.

Meanwhile, Sir Charles and Miss Courtenay were standing upon the way side, in as profound silence as if they were actually the spectres, for whom a wayfaring man would have mistaken them. Constance, on finding herself safe, was unable to

refrain from giving way to a burst of tears, to
which thankfulness for her deliverance, and
agitation at the novelty of her situation, im-
pelled her. Gentlemanly in every action, Sir
Charles appeared unconscious of this necessary
relief, to a timid, and feminine, but not weak,
or cowardly mind. After some minutes' silence,
he entreated her to allow him to protect her
from the damps of night with his own riding
cloak, every incumbrance in the shape of enve-
lopes having been left by her in the carriage,
in order to facilitate her release. This proposal was silently accepted by Constance, who
was ashamed of her own dismantled appearance, her white dress waving to the wind, and
her head uncovered, standing too, in the dead
of night, apart from others, with a young
stranger. The next entreaty of the Baronet
was, that she would avail herself of the support
of his arm, for he could not, he said, but perceive the tremulousness which this frightful ad-
venture had occasioned in her, and he trusted
that she would excuse the seeming liberty taken
by so recent an acquaintance, and accept of his
aid. But whilst all this gallantry was going

forward, Mr. Bouverie, released from his less captivating charge, and dismounted from his horse, made his way up to Sir Charles with Miss Courtenay, and, cruelly for his friend, frustrated the opportunity of making himself agreeable, which fortune had chalked out for him. He informed Miss Courtenay, with extreme modesty of manner, " that it had been 'arranged by the conclave in the mourning coach, that they would make room for her, their vehicle being fortunately of an ample size; it was also decided that he and Sir Charles should perform the office of piloting Mr. Cattell's chariot home, and prevent the drenched votary of Bacchus from effecting any further mischief. Chilled, and weary, Constance had scarcely warmth enough left in her to be grateful, even to Sir Charles. She endeavoured, indeed, to speak her acknowledgements, but with feminine contrariety, thanked Mr. Bouverie most, and left Sir Charles with scarcely the reward of a civil word. Yet hers was neither a nature to forget benefits, nor to feel injuries slightly, and it was, in this instance, the vehemence of her feelings, which checked

what she might have uttered. Much emula-
tion was displayed by the two gentlemen, as
to which should have the honour of replacing
on her fair shoulders her own mantle, which
had been restored to her; which operation
being completed, Constance was soon received
within the warm precincts of a coach, containing eight people. Many condolences were
passed on all sides. The middle-aged Miss
Grey was fearful that her dear friend Miss
Monckton would have her old, troublesome
cough again. Miss Pearson calculated the
depth to which the carriage must have sunk,
and might have sunk, still farther. Her cousin, a pretty blue-eyed young lady, declared, she considered Sir Charles the " first
of men," and said, with a sigh, that she
thought him like Lord St. Orville, in Eve-
lina. Miss Monckton, at this remark, revived
a little, and observed that Miss Courtenay
might remember " that she owed her life to
him." This admonition was received in silence, which was only broken by Mrs. Crawfurd, a widow lady, declaring, " that for her
part, she would never go to a dance in a
Mourning Coach again."

CHAPTER V.

Slander prevails! to woman's longing mind,
Sweet as the April blossom to the bee.
                    Hogg—*Mador of the Moor.*

On the following days sundry reports ran round
the town of Newberry, of a nature very re-
volting to the delicacy of Miss Monckton.
Some related, that in the hurry of escaping,
one of her shoes came off; (the days of sandals
not being then arrived;) others, that she had
fainted away in the arms of Mr. Bouverie, who
was obliged to call Sir Charles to his aid, to
assist him in holding her. In short, such ill-
natured things were said, that the calumniated
lady had some thoughts of contradicting them
in a circular to her friends. Neither did Miss
Courtenay escape. By the pretenders to kind,
compassionate interest in the young lady, it was
lamented, that Mr. Bouverie, to whom she had

shown so evident a partiality during the evening, should not have been her deliverer instead
of Sir Charles. All agreed that she was
" making a dead set at him;" but, according
to the opinions of several staid damsels, turned
thirty, he was too sensible, high-minded and
pious, to be taken by a pretty face, and a girl
of seventeen. Ah, ladies! your knowledge of
human nature was but scanty !

Meanwhile, Constance had begun much to reproach herself for the apparent indifference she
had displayed to the obligations received from Sir
Charles. She endeavoured, in the course of a long
morning call from Mr. Bouverie, to introduce
the subject, and to show some sense of gratitude,
in hopes that it might " go round" to his
friend : but Mr. Bouverie had so much to say
on general subjects, after his first inquiries
had been answered, he had so many new books
to recommend to Miss Courtenay, he could
point out so many views in the vicinity, subjects for her pencil, and he ran over the various
pursuits of botany, poetry, history, and con-
chology, so rapidly, and with so little intermis-
sion, that Constance could not interrupt him in

his progress to make a studied, and perhaps unexpected eulogium upon his friend's exertion. Yet Mr. Bouverie was not considered a great talker : it was, however, remarked that in Miss Courtenay's presence he became so. This, it was presumed, was the first stage of love—like a fever, which quickly rises to delirium—then comes the low, agitated, pensive, silent state; lastly, the certainty either of present cure, or speedy death. But nobody in Newberry at that time, dreamed of anything like annihilation to Mr. Bouverie's hopes.

Constance resolved, that the very first time she should have an opportunity of speaking to Sir Charles, she would endeavour to make him sensible of her gratitude. To this she was further incited by the reproaches of Miss Monckton, who told her that she had behaved shamefully, inexcusably, and assured her that she knew Sir Charles had too much proper pride ever to do any thing but slightly bow to her in future; not that the good lady thought this in her heart, but she was really anxious that her favourite young beau, Sir Charles, should meet with some little return for his ardent admi-

ration of Miss Courtenay.   Little did this
well-intentioned woman dream of the woes
which she might be preparing for both parties, by creating in either an interest, which,
in young minds, is seldom devoid of some portion of the romantic.   But it is remarked, that
no persons are so fond of meddling in love affairs, as those who have nothing to do with
them themselves.

Due notice having been given of a Card
party, at the house of Mrs. De Courcy, an
acquaintance of Mrs. Cattell's, Constance was
certain, that she should meet Sir Charles there,
and was resolved to behave as well as her natural courage, and a foolish habit of blushing,
from which, in the progress of human intellect, our more modern young ladies are happily exempt, would allow her.   She therefore screwed her courage to the sticking place,
and arranged, during sundry successive reveries, a very proper, modest, yet somewhat
flattering address to the young Baronet.   She
felt secure that he would be at Mrs. De
Courcy's, because, not only was he always invited to every party given by the haut ton of

Newberry; but because, also, he was supposed
to be rather intimate with the lady hostess of
the projected rout. For Mrs. De Courcy was
not a widow after the fashion of half-mourning,
lilac and black ribbons, and a perpetual black
silk gown; but a pretty, accomplished woman
of thirty, who patronized the circulating libra-
ries, had her bonnets from London, improved
upon Nature with a little rouge, flirted when
she had an opportunity, but was select in
her flirtations. She was fond of poetry, drew a
little, sang a little, and walked about a good
deal; was observed to be partial to the elm
walk in the Priory Park, drove a pony phaeton,
and was sometimes overtaken by Sir Charles,
and, in short, was supposed not to dislike him.
Constance, had she designed to captivate the
" observed of all observers" in the town of
Newberry, would never have thought of entering the lists with so practised a flirt as Mrs. De
Courcy, by universal and sedulous report of all
ladies of inferior attractions, was noted to be.
The sole aim of the simple-minded girl was,
as she thought, to do what she ought to have
done before; but it is a matter of conjecture,

whether if her deliverer had been the good-looking Mr. Thomas Tribe, or the man of figure, his brother, instead of Sir Charles Marchmont, she would have thought quite so much of the mode of conveying her thanks.

At length the evening, and the sedan arrived, in which first Mrs. Cattell and then Miss Courtenay were to be conveyed to a Newberry rout. Constance was dressed, on this occasion, with great simplicity, and in a style almost girlish, yet she found far more trouble than heretofore in arranging her attire to her satisfaction. Her hair was impracticable, her frock too short-waisted, and she, who was generally dressed with much dispatch, was, on this occasion, almost as long at her toilet, as old Mrs. Cattell. Yet, as she descended the stairs, Vandyck, could he have stepped out of his grave to have seen her, might have deemed a portrait of her, a fit companion for that loveliest of nature's works,—Henrietta Maria of England. Like that justly celebrated beauty, the features of Constance possessed elevation, chastened by extreme delicacy. Her redundant hair, which, arranged in fifty various ways, still became

her, was, in colour and glossiness, not unlike
the rich brown hues in the plumage of a phea-
sant, although somewhat darker. Its clustering curls hung upon a brow where innocence
contended with intelligence, which should
stamp its character most forcibly. The dark
blue eye beneath, was totally devoid of that
flash and glare which are thought by vulgar
judges to constitute what are called fine eyes ;
and never, under any circumstances, lost the
softness of their expression, although that expression were alternated by thought, or by
mirth, or by sorrow. Few could look into
those eyes without sympathy with every feeling
which they indicated ; few who had long been
accustomed to view them, could forget the de-
licious repose, the exquisite playfulness by
which they were varied, and characterized.—
To complete the sketch. The figure of Miss
Courtenay had at this time almost attained its
full stature, but not its subsequent dimensions.
Gently restrained, but not confined by dress,
it had scarcely attained the form or rotundity
of womanhood. Its slightness and activity
were, however, unmarked by angularity, and

its flexibility and beautiful proportions gave promise, in this budding stage between youth and maturity, of future perfection of womanly grace. Such was the outline of her person; and the whole was rendered interesting to the intelligent observer, not only by the total absence of all artifice, and of that accomplishment which is called "making the most of oneself;" but by a refinement, and involuntary display of habitual good-breeding, which, whilst it was natural to Constance, had undoubtedly been confirmed and improved, not by art, but by habit and imitation.

This digression, whilst Mrs. Cattell is entering her chair, must be excused, because it is presumed that none of my readers will be very anxious to know the particulars of that lady's appearance. Neither will Mr. Cattell's mushroom wig, black satin breeches, and large buckles, be here expatiated upon, though, relatively to him, subjects of no small concern.

Constance entered Mrs. De Courcy's drawing-room full of good resolutions. Sir Charles, however, appeared not. Mr. Bouverie was the only gentleman that broke the unspeckled white of a large circle of ladies in muslin dresses, who were sipping their tea out of little china cups without handles, or ladling the cream out of a little silver vase, formerly in vogue before the less elaborate use of the cream-jug came into fashion. Meanwhile, pools of quadrille, rubbers of cassino, and hands of whist were formed, to the exclusion only of Constance, who could not play, and of Mr. Bouverie, who never played. Sly glances were exchanged between some of the partners, and stupid old Mrs. Cattell was observed once to look round, as Mr. Bouverie took his place by Miss Courtenay. But Constance, almost to her own surprise, was disconcerted at the non-appearance of Sir Charles, without liking to ask if there were any chance of his arrival. "Well!" thought she, with some vexation, "he must continue to think me ungrateful, that is all." Every time the neat little footboy opened the door, she expected to see him enter, but every time was disappointed. Only once was his name mentioned, when, in answer to an apparently careless inquiry from Mrs. De Courcy, Mr. Bouverie informed the listening circle, that "he had gone into Leicestershire that morning;

upon which Miss Pearson, and two elderly
ladies, the Miss Seagraves, interchanged looks,
with a sort of running glance at Mrs. De Courcy,
significant of the disappointment which they
supposed that lady to feel; but the attention of
the younger portion of the assemblage was
wholly engrossed by the close siege which they
now conceived Mr. Bouverie to be laying to Miss
Courtenay's heart; for in Newberry, where
few were the opportunities afforded to the fair
sex of witnessing the course of " true love," a
civil bow was deemed a sort of matrimonial
prelude; the offer of an arm considered as a
symptom of a speedy wedding; and two or three
polite speeches from a gentleman to a lady, set
the whole town in an agitation.

CHAPTER VI.

She is a woman, and she may be woo'd,
She is a woman, and she may be won.

SHAKSPEARE.

IN the course of a few weeks, Constance was taken by Mr. and Mrs. Cattell to pay their annual visit to Powis Court, an old manor house about six miles from Newberry. It was a specimen of the imposing and picturesque architecture, in which the English gentry and nobility spent some of the wealth which they had in many instances acquired in foreign wars, in the reign of Queen Elizabeth. Like most of the works of her time, Powis Court was stately and enduring, without any great appearance of strength and massiveness. The front was regular, and somewhat castellated,

E 2

with every possible variety in the shape and size of its windows; but the back and sides of the building jutted into numerous gable ends and compartments. Its fair but not extensive domains, assorted well with the mansion. A broad and exquisitely rolled, gravelled space in front, without the vestige of a weed or the apprehension of a loose stone, was succeeded by an ever verdant lawn sloping upwards, and gradually narrowing into an avenue of pines, which extended to the belt by which the pleasure-grounds were enclosed. To the right and to the left of the house, were groves of Plane, Acacia, Hawthorn, Sycamore, and Lignum Vitæ, thronged with those tuneful inhabitants which serve as companions to the meditative rambler, and intersected by many walks, which seemed to hold out lures for duets of an equally fond description with those diligently pursued by the feathered denizens of the " bosky dell." The woods, now faintly touched with autumnal hues, extended on the one hand to the high road, on the other to a well-managed, over-stocked, garden.

The former mistress of this fair demesne, was a Mrs. Powis; but she had very lately resigned her sovereign controul to her son, recently of age, and acted, with deference to his superior right, as the nominal director only of the concerns of Powis Court. She was a good, useful, and cheerful, widow lady; hospitable to a proverb, notable beyond imitation, and charitable almost to a fault. By her excessive love of order, a virtue now quite out of date, the interior of Powis Court had been kept up during the long minority of her son, with a nicety which is almost inconceivable in a modern house. Acting as trustee for the heir of Powis Court, every item of furniture, every old picture or print, every window-curtain and counterpane, had been transmitted to him on his birthday in marvellous preservation. All savoured of the antique; and Mr. Powis was little likely, if report spoke true, to remodel the ancient edifice, or to furnish anew the old seat of his ancestors.

Mr. Powis, of Powis Court, had never for a single instant of his boyhood or youth, forgotten that he was his own important self. His

family genealogy hung in the hall, his family
monuments stood before him in the church.
His mother, for the honour of the family, had
always made a marked distinction between him
and his younger brother; in short, she had
petted him, coddled him, and humoured him,
till he became more like a girl than a boy.
His little, irritable, proud, selfish mind settled
upon trifles; and being almost always with
elderly ladies, he had imbibed all their dawdling,
gossiping ways, thought their occupations of
paramount importance, and, when he went to
college, made his own chair-covers, and employed some hours in cutting out fly-catchers.
He had quitted Oxford without making a single
acquaintance, and having acquired nothing but
additional habits of unemployed seclusion, and
of indolent retirement. Strange to say, he had
also returned with increased ideas of his own
personal importance, and of the importance of
Powis Court. He was now installed in the full
dignity of possession.

It was inwardly thought by Mrs. Cattell to
be a point of propriety to introduce her charge
to the notice of this interesting young free-

holder; not that she had the remotest thoughts
of love on either side. Of that passion she knew
only the forms; she was acquainted with it
only as the tie which bound Jacob to Rachel,
or as the motive which brought Sir Charles
Grandison forward in full dress, bowing away
like a Chinese mandarin. But Mrs. Cattell
had much respect for the institution of marriage, which she could fully comprehend, because she had entered into it with Mr. Cattell,
but she had not the remotest conception of any
thing beyond the scope of his actions. Constance had, however, nothing to fear or to hope
from the young heir, who thought far more of
a game of piquet with Mrs. Cattell herself,
than of a flirtation with her young ward. He
received them, indeed, in the room of his
mother, who was, at the moment of their arrival, inspecting the progress of some damson
cheese; and he conducted his guests into a sitting apartment coldly blue, and awfully tidy,
into which, as it was not yet Michaelmas, the
introduction of a fire had not been permitted.
Here they sat, receiving the condescending as-
siduities of the youth, who, like a newly created

peer, thought it incumbent upon him to be particularly condescending; until the half-hour dinner-bell sounded, when Constance and her aged friend retired to their several apartments to dress.

The circle at Powis Court was at this time unusually cheerful, compared with the assemblage of elderly gentlemen and ladies who usually composed it, for Mrs. Powis's chief acquaintance were sexagenarians, like her deceased husband, who had been much older than herself. Antiquated virgins of good family, who came to spend a long day with her, and prosing old squires and their wives, who strolled about the grounds whilst their horses were put up, formed the chief part of her society.

At the present season, however, there were two young visitors at Powis Court, before Constance arrived there. The first, by courtesy, to be described of these, was Miss Letitia Sperling, the niece of Mrs. Powis, but otherwise, as her aunt herself observed, " no ways remarkable." She was a tall, insipid girl, with a back like a deal-board, and long, angular limbs, unfledged as it were, and till now not emancipated from the parent nest, and was compared by Miss Monckton to a "darning needle." Her character must be detailed in negatives: she was not pretty, she was not lively, she was not well-bred, she was not entertaining, she was not useful. We would willingly consign her to oblivion, but that every human being, whether gifted or not, has some part to perform in life. At present, she seemed to answer no earthly purpose but to afford Mrs. Powis the privilege of saying, "that she had a *young* lady at Powis Court."

The other inmate was Captain Edmund Powis, the half-brother of Mrs. Powis's defunct husband, and heir to all the poverty, obscurity, and temptations to bad passions, which seem entailed on the younger sons of opulence. He was also that anomalous being, a modest soldier: his diffidence, which probably proceeded from his early dependence on an elder brother, was the more remarkable when opposed to the acknowledged courage in the field which had raised him, without interest, to his present rank. To the fair sex he was peculiarly re-

served, and never, by his nearest relations, had
he been suspected of the remotest dream of an
attachment. In age, he was about five and
and thirty, and his appearance, matured by
time, and improved by personal activity, presented a fine contrast to that of his half-
nephew.

The most remarkable trait about this brave
officer was his taciturnity; yet, to the nice observer, he might seem not deficient in soldier-
like knowledge, nor insensible to the pleasures
of the belles lettres. A handsome, regular, but
somewhat unvarying physiognomy, and a gentlemanly deportment, complete the portrait. Sim-
ple-hearted, and kind herself, Constance was
almost instantly struck by the evident small
account in which Captain Powis was held by his
relations at Powis Court. Mrs. Powis was, indeed, too good-natured not to evince the utmost
hospitality to every one under her roof; but her
eyes, her ears, her thoughts, were engrossed
with her eldest son; and she seemed to assign
the superiority to him in all things, as un-
hesitatingly as the vassals in feudal times to
their chiefs. The precious favourite himself

lost no opportunity of showing off his own little pride, and Constance could sometimes with pleasure have left the room when he talked to " uncle Edmund" of "my horses," "my farms," " my rents," " my gardens," " my tenants," " my bailiffs," &c. Neither could she forbear expressing to Mrs. Cattell the futile wish that destiny had made the captain the heir of Powis Court, and his effeminate relative, not a soldier — for he was only fit to war with women—but at any rate a younger son: but such a declaration on her part was considered by Mrs. Cattell as little better than very profane talking. " Hyperion to a satyr," thought Constance, as she one day compared the two kinsmen ; the one erect, and full grown, with the bending, unmuscular, thread-paper like form of the other. Meanwhile, artless herself, and unsuspicious of the observations of others, she often endeavoured, though in vain, to draw the retiring and neglected Edmund out of the obstinate silence in which he generally persevered.

The system maintained at Powis Court was not conducive to the acceleration of intimacies, nor kindly favourable to flirtations. A strict separation of the ladies and gentlemen, except at meal times, was the order of the day. After a stately breakfast, Captain Powis, whose visit was with the express purpose of shooting, and who was thought to be highly favoured in being permitted such a privilege, withdrew to his sports, and was seldom visible till dinner time. The lord of the manor himself dawdled about the flower beds, or wrangled with the servants, or wrote in red ink little conundrums, or worried the patience of his grooms, or took a languid ride; and so he was disposed of. Constance, who was at that buoyant age when the mind can almost create its own world, was perfectly contented by the prospect of a walk, even with companions so totally uninteresting as Miss Sperling and William Powis. She walked between them, enjoyed the rich scenery, wished for her sketch-book, and longed to have her sister with her.

The vicinity of Powis Court was wild and unfrequented, and though the young pedestrians frequently heard the guns of the sportsmen, they seldom, in their rambles, came in

contact with a human being. It is in such
excursions as these that our love of nature is
put to the test; the assistance of the imagination is called into play, and the mind, even
of the gay and thoughtless, forced into reflection.

An incident, however, soon occurred, to vary
the scene. " My son expects Sir Charles
Marchmont and Mr. Bouverie to-day," said
Mrs. Powis, one morning at breakfast; " Miss
Monckton is coming also, and Sir Charles
offered her a place in his chariot, which of
course she declined; for that, you know,"
looking · at Mrs. Cattell, " would not be
proper."

" Would not be proper indeed," echoed that
lady.

" Not proper, mama !" said William, a forward boy; "why, I should think Miss Monckton might have come with *him,* for she is old
enough to be his mother."

"Be quiet, William," said Mrs. Powis; "you
are too young to judge of those things; wait
till you have seen as much of society as your
brother my dear."

" But if I were to see society for ever," replied the youth, " it would never make me think
Miss Monckton young—or that it could be
improper for her to come along with Sir
Charles. Why, you would not call it improper
for Miss Courtenay to go in a post-chaise with
my uncle Edmund, and he's about the age of
Miss Monckton, and she's quite a girl."

" I beg you will not make free with Miss
Courtenay's age, William," returned Mrs.
Powis.

" Nor with mine either," said Captain Powis,
in a tone scarcely audible; the first words
which he had been known to speak in full conclave.

" What spirits William has, ma'am," sighed
forth the elder brother; " but no wonder, he
has not the cares which I have."

" No, my dear, very true, he has not your
cares upon him; a large property is a very
great care, is it not, Mrs. Cattell?"

" Very great, very great indeed," returned
the old lady in a tone of condolence.

" I should like to try," observed William,
drily.

" Well, young gentlemen! you will be ready to receive your guests; I mean *your* guests, Mr. Powis," said Mrs. Powis as she quitted the room, " at four o'clock'; Sir Charles has set his mind on a stroll with Mrs. Cattell round the lawn before dinner ; so he says in his note."

" He has a horrid bad taste then," whispered William to Miss Sperling, " for she walks so remarkably slow. I pitted her against the Canada goose the other day, and the goose gained it by three minutes."

Notwithstanding the risk which Sir Charles ran of being beaten by the Canada goose also, if he chose to undertake a *tête-a-tête* with Mrs. Catell, he came in time to walk with her ; and to punish him for his insincerity, he found Mrs. Cattell quite prepared to take him at his word, and to accompany him round the grounds In vain he looked up every alley, and into every arbour, in hopes of seeing the pretty object of his visit, who, he had the vanity to flatter himself, would really put herself in his way. She had gone in another direction, on horseback with William, and returned only just in time for dinner, and scarcely in time to dress. Meanwhile the young Baronet exhausted his agreeable spirits, and soiled his shoes, casting his " bread upon the waters," and addressing himself in vain to his stupid companion, who was about as intellectual as the trees and shrubs amongst which they wandered. He thought the dinner-bell would never ring, and not being able, by his indirect questions, to extract from the dull old lady a positive answer whether Miss Courtenay were at Powis Court or not, was once half inclined to order his carriage and drive away.

From this act of despair he was saved by the entrance of Mr. Bouverie, who, in the happy guilelessness of a heart at ease, asked boldly how Miss Courtenay was, and if they were to have the pleasure of seeing her to-day.

" Why, yes," said Mrs. Cattell; " she's somewhere with her young companions, for she's vastly fond of that Miss Sperling, I believe; and I dare say they're both with the Captain !"

Here was a piece of intelligence !

" What Captain ?" asked Sir Charles of Mr.

Bouverie, and "O! what a place to make love in! I declare I thought these groves looked as if they were haunted by muses or by lovers! Here's a seat underneath that tree just fit for two people; the walks are only wide enough for two—nature and art alike seem resolved upon a *tête-a-tête.* 'O happy shades! to me unblest!' These captains ought to be extirpated! There's a race of them everywhere. Ask a pretty girl to dance with you, and she's engaged to the captain! No matter whether a long-legged Irish captain of militia, or a squat Birmingham volunteer officer, who made the arms which he brandishes; if he be but a captain, that's enough! Well, who do you suppose this invincible captain to be?"

"O," replied Mr. Bouverie, "he is only a relation of the family, a brave officer in the artillery; not one of the equivocal sort of zoophites, connecting links between the civil and military condition, upon which useful class of people you are pleased to be so severe."

"And is he young?" asked Sir Charles.

"About thirty-three," answered the Vicar.

"Oh Heavens! the most dangerous age.— And handsome?"

"I believe he is considered so," said his friend.

"Agreeable?"

"Yes."

"And rich?"

"Why, no."

"No: that's some consolation! But *malheur a moi!* that does not much signify either, for at seventeen, girls are not so clever at compound addition as seven years afterwards; or at any rate, they cast up the sum of a man's personal qualifications, and make their calculations somewhat after this fashion:—fine eyes they will set down against a fine estate; good teeth they will take in preference to a good house; flattering and tender looks, the disinterested little creatures will value at a much higher price than a long purse; and a little sentimentality, more especially, Bouverie, if there be a touch of religion in it, a something between Rousseau and Fenelon—makes them forget all the pounds, shillings, and pence in the kingdom. But come; do let us go in, and reconnoitre our costume a little: don't let the captain have all the advantage. I dare say the fellow is a mere block to hang regimentals on; a walking ramrod—a piece of humanity faced with a yard or two of scarlet cloth," continued the thoughtless young baronet, as they entered the house.

It sometimes happens that a young and beautiful woman appears to far greater advantage when she is hastily, and even carelessly dressed, than when the utmost pains have been bestowed upon her appearance. So was it with Constance on this occasion. Knowing the excessive precision of her host and hostess, and being extremely considerate with respect to the wishes and arrangements of others, a good property out of date now, she was almost breathless, from her haste to complete her toilette; when she reached the drawing-room door, the last bell had sounded, and the company were just at the critical moment of departure. Mr. Cattell held Mrs. Powis by the tip of his little finger, after the fashion of former days, looking as if he were afraid to touch her; the young host was

marching out with Mrs. Cattell; Mr. Bouverie
had resigned himself to Miss Monckton; Sir
Charles, who ought to have led the van, having
waited dexterously in an embrasure, `talking
with such pretended earnestness to William,
that no one chose to interrupt him. When
Constance entered, the Baronet came, however, to a sudden period in his discourse,
and moved quickly forward to offer her his
hand. Before he could, with all his speed,
reach her, she had consigned herself to the care
of the Captain, who, whether intentionally or
not could not be known, had intercepted her
on her entrance. Too gentlemanly to insist
upon his right, the countenance of Sir Charles
was yet overclouded by vexation, and he followed, with a far less agreeable aspect than was
his wont. Few of our readers will pity him,
for they will naturally conclude that his admiration of a lovely and unprotected girl was
far more the result of a selfish desire of transitory amusement, than of any feelings which
could terminate in the rational happiness of
either party. Yet, if we allow this conjecture
to be true, it must also be granted, that Sir

Charles was neither a practised flirt nor a designing libertine. Too easily captivated by
beauty, or by grace, he was seldom known to
accord to it more than the common attentions
of gallantry, unless when there existed along
with personal charms corresponding elegance
of mind; or, what is still more likely to allure
vain man, a decided preference to himself; a
circumstance which even to the latest day of
life, has a most powerful influence on all men.
He was now, however, piqued in no small
degree, at the indifference which Miss Courtenay
appeared to evince towards him. To others she
was easy, and sometimes playful, but towards
him she seldom looked, nor ever voluntarily
addressed him. He also remarked, with some
chagrin, that she never alluded even distantly,
though now in his presence for the first time,
to the evening when he saved her from a peril,
at once imminent and ignoble. On the other
hand, Constance was abashed and displeased at
the undisguised, and as she thought, impertinent admiration which he evinced of her personal
qualifications, which, it must be remembered,

were the more conspicuous when set off by such foils as Miss Monckton, Mrs. Cattell, Miss Sperling, and Mrs. Powis. She thought he had no right to make her the object of his undisguised attention, and almost wished herself at school again, rather than be condemned to encounter what she had good taste enough to consider as an insult. She could but acknowledge that he was infinitely superior to the rest of the company in information, in natural wit, and in manners; and even Mr. Bouverie appeared deficient in ease and vivacity, in comparison with his accomplished friend. Such is the charm of good breeding, and so powerful an influence has it in setting off our best qualities, that even whilst she disliked Sir Charles, she admired his deportment. Once or twice she determined to address him, and to thank him for his timely services to her on the fatal mourning-coach business; but whenever she looked towards him, she encountered in his eyes such an expression as men of the world study to throw into their countenances when they wish to show their admiration of the other sex; and being new to this species of notice, and naturally susceptible of the slightest impropriety, Constance felt that she could not speak to her unabashed admirer.

Meanwhile, as dinner proceeded, Sir Charles experienced from Miss Monckton, some of that private, gentle castigation with which that lady occasionally indulged her particular friends.

" My dear Miss Monckton," said he, " how happy I was to see you safe from that execrable dilemma in which you were placed the other night."

" You might be happy to see me safe," returned she, " but you did nothing to help me out of it."

" But you know you had my best wishes," rejoined Sir Charles; " and besides, I was occupied in saving one very dear to you; and you may conceive how much it grieved me that I could not act as the personal liberator of both."

" You are very kind. I always find that we elderly ladies have the best wishes of such young gallants as you—we have apologies instead of services, and polite speeches enough, if we will keep out of your way. But I forgive you—Miss Courtenay is a *fair* excuse for you."

" Indeed she is—fair as Iceland snows, and as cold, as some one has said; she is lovely, but wants soul; her loveliness will never cause one pang in any man's heart; no one can adore a statue; nor did any man ever shoot himself for an automaton."

" Statue! automaton! This shows your discernment indeed, Sir Charles. You want to make a fool of the girl, and find her insensible to the gross flattery with which you fine gentlemen assail beauty. You quarrel with her because she is too modest to encourage your advances. Reverse the picture; suppose that she met you with the assurance of a woman of fashion, or the pert boldness of a vulgar rustic, what would you think of her—say of her? Are not you men the first to fling incense on the shrine of vanity, and the first to ridicule her votaries? Is it not your daily aim to lead on poor victims to folly, and then to punish them with scorn?"

" But, my dear Miss Moncton, how serious a view you are taking ——"

" By no means too serious; many are the

young women whose characters are ruined, though not in the common acceptation of the word, on their first coming into society. The weak and selfish let them pass—no one cares for them; but the affectionate, the generous, the confiding, the gay and innocent, are assailed with attentions which mean nothing, but which have serious, though varied, effects upon all of them. A taste for excitement is given—in some instances the heart is entangled—the common duties of life, its rational occupations become vapid—all moral and mental improvement is at an end—one object alone is kept in view, and that is admiration. A parent cannot teach the young heart to distrust, but must, I fear, in many instances see its best affections withered, and the highest faculties of the mind unemployed, and all—all for the gratification of man's vanity; for I will not call it by a worse name. But the ladies are rising, and I must leave you to digest my lecture, or to laugh at it, whichever you think best."

The evening was sultry, and Constance, after breathing for some time the air of that suffocating atmosphere of formality, a ladies'

drawing room after dinner, grew weary o
Mrs. Powis's eulogiums upon her son and her ser
vants, of Mrs. Cattell's dozing replies, an
even of the acrid seasoning with which Mis
Monckton's conversation was interspersed. It
was now about the middle of September, and
the dinner-hour at Powis Court being foui
precisely, there was still daylight sufficient to
tempt the young and active to an evening stroll.
Constance stood, her feet resting on the thresh-
hold of the drawing-room window, and contemplating with a longing view the face o
nature in that deadly repose which sometimes
precedes its wildest convulsions. Not a breath
moved the high tops of the Larches, or ruffled
the delicate foliage of the Acacias. The feathered tribe were silent, and a solemn stillness,
"save where the beetle wheeled his drony flight,"
attended the last rays of sun-set. Constance long·
ed, like the " owl," to " complain" to the moon
of the imprisonment to which she compared her
present situation—confined in a dull drawing-
room, with still duller companions. With the
exquisite " Ode on Evening" of one of our most
faultless poets in her thoughts, she glided from

the presence of the junto, and entangling Miss Sperling, whom she met at the door, in her scheme, proposed a walk to the summer-house at the end of the avenue. Miss Sperling was one of those giggling girls who love a joke in a dull way; she could comprehend nothing that was not practical; delicate shades of humour were thrown away upon her, but a trick, or a valentine, were quite upon the level of her capacity. She entered immediately into the idea; and cloakless, and bonnetless, they pursued their way to the spot proposed, Constance enjoying her emancipation, and Miss Sperling laughing, and wondering whether her cousin William would find her out. As they proceeded, the wind rose, at first not more than sufficient to blow back the ringlets of their hair, and to induce Constance to raise her head joyously to receive the freshening breeze; but as they approached the summer-house, a hurricane, which made the woods resound, and whistled through the old avenue, warned them of the approaching storm. They had scarcely begun to retrace their steps, when a loud, and near clap of thunder, succeeded by vivid light-

nings, transfixed them both with fear; but a
violent shower of rain coming on, they hastened
into the summer-house, too glad to gain that
dangerous station, as a shelter.

In the mean time, the gentlemen having perceived the storm, had risen hastily from their
wine, and the party being thus disturbed, soon
adjourned to the drawing-room. Here they found
a general desertion on the part of their female
friends had taken place. Mrs. Cattell and
Mrs. Powis had retreated to the cellar, and
Miss Monckton, equally alarmed with themselves, had gone to bed. The young ladies
were no where to be seen. It was supposed
that they had also concealed themselves, and
the gentlemen, who had borne the absconding
of the elder ladies with great fortitude, and
had never, to do them justice, even talked of
following Mrs. Cattell and Mrs. Powis to the
cellar, began their search for the younger
nymphs with great eagerness. They might be
in the library—an instant investigation of that
apartment was made, but no living being was
visible among the lettered dead; and to say
the truth, seldom was the repose of those heroes

disturbed at Powis Court. The billiard-room, the keeping-room, as it was called in old-fashioned times, (a sort of steward's room,) were also inspected. It was concluded that they also had retired to their separate apartments, and Sir Charles, who had been ringleader in the search, returned to the drawing-room, followed by Mr. Bouverie and Captain Powis, each evincing, according to their different characters, differing expressions of disappointment in their countenances. Meanwhile, the fury of the storm was such, that the old building seemed to rock to its foundations, and few, even of the stoutest hearted, could view, without awe, the visible effects of the power of Him whose voice is in the whirlwind. On a sudden, after a private intimation from William Powis, Sir Charles started up in some agitation, and hastened to the lawn. His departure was not observed by Mr. Bouverie, who was contemplating, with mingled feelings, the warfare of the elements; but Captain Powis instantly followed the Baronet. He saw Sir Charles flying with the utmost speed in the direction of the summer-house, with his cloak hanging over his arm, regardless of the heavy rain which had now succeeded the thunder and lightning. It is difficult to say which of the two young men ran with the greatest eagerness. They entered the summer-house almost at the same time. They found Miss Sperling extended on the floor, in a state of insensibility; the roof of the little edifice was secured with cramps of iron, and the electrical fluid, without causing any fatal effect, had produced in the poor girl all the semblance of death. Beside her was Constance, pale as the statue to which Sir Charles had compared her, supporting upon her knees the head of her companion, and with an expression in her countenance of despair, in aggravating which self-reproach played a busy part. Destined, as it seemed, by the performance of offices of kindness, to dispel her prejudices towards him, Sir Charles earnestly, yet gently entreated her to resign to him the lifeless burden which she held, and to escape immediately to the house. At his approach Constance raised her eyes, which had been intently fixed upon Miss Sperling; but as she saw alarm strongly depicted in Sir Charles's countenance, the thought flashed across her that he saw the hand of death depicted on the countenance of her young companion. In an agony of self-accusation, she exclaimed,

" O, Sir Charles, you are come too late! It was I—it was I who brought her here: may God forgive me!" and leaning her head on the seat of the summer-house, she gave vent to a passionate burst of anguish, such as the first sorrows of youth produce in a sensitive mind. Sir Charles, though full of vivacity, and even deemed reckless by his friends, was a man of excellent and warm feelings. With the utmost tenderness of manner he endeavoured to reassure her; and with the assistance of Captain Powis, who lent a *silent* aid, he raised the sufferer from the position in which she had lain, and placed her on the seat; he pointed out the symptoms of returning animation, and entreated Miss Courtenay to return to the house; for, said he, " There *is* danger here," and he entreated her to leave him to follow with Miss Sperling. But Constance resolutely refused to quit her companion: " I have brought her into this," she said, " and I will not desert her—my inexperience, my ignorance plead my excuse; but see, Captain Powis is gone; he will return with assistance."

"Dear Miss Courtenay," said Sir Charles, do not reproach yourself, your friend will be restored to you, and you—rescued from this danger, will be more valued, will be dearer to your friends than ever." These words were said with a softness of manner, which would, at any other time, have overwhelmed poor Constance with confusion.

"But see, see!" said she, "she revives—" tell me, tell me, how you feel;" eagerly inquired she, as Miss Sperling looked round her, and extended her hand.—"She is only stunned. Thank God!" exclaimed Constance; her warm heart glowing to Him who had been a present help in trouble. "And you, Sir Charles;" said she, her lively affections expanding to human objects, "you have saved me before, and I did not thank you—forgive me, and believe that I shall never forget your kindness," she added, the blood rushing to her cheeks as she spoke; whilst in the ardour of the moment, she half extended her hand towards him. She withdrew it, however, on hearing footsteps, so instinctive, even in our most excited moments, is the sense of propriety in a pure female mind; but Sir Charles was resolved not to be cheated of the half-proffered favour. He pressed respectfully, but somewhat warmly, the pledge of gratitude; but his manner was far more modest, and respectful, than it had hitherto been; for he knew how to combine, most happily, an expression of fervent admiration towards one object, with that of the utmost reverence. Meanwhile, servants, cloaks, and condolences arrived in profusion : a sort of litter was formed for Miss Sperling, by the united arms of the old butler, the two housemaids, and the dairy-maid. Covered with every variety of wrapper, and looking like a bundle of shawls, she was carried down the avenue, and Constance, wrapped in a thick Spanish mantilla of Sir Charles's, and leaning on his arm and that of Captain Powis regained the drawing-room.

CHAPTER VII.

O ! lost to virtue, lost to manly thought,
Lost to the noble sallies of the soul ;
Who think it solitude to be alone.—YOUNG.

Brushing, with hasty steps, the dew away.—GRAY.

To those of my readers who may be very
anxious about the recovery of Miss Sperling,
it may be satisfactory to learn, that by dint of
lavender drops, gruel, warm bottles, cooling
draughts, much pity, and plenty of her favourite remedy, sleep, the young lady was
actually in tolerable health the next day, but, by
her own acknowledgment, on the road only to
convalescence a week afterwards; for she was
one of those persons, who having no other
earthly importance, are fond of the distinction
that a little illness gives them, and always keep
up the game to the last. Constance was very
attentive to her, and by force of sympathy, would

have become attached to her, had there been a single loveable property in Miss Sperling. They parted, nevertheless, with mutual regret, when the full period allowed for Mrs. Cattell's visit being completed, Constance bade adieu to Powis Court. But there was one person, who, without altering a muscle of his countenance, experienced sincere concern at the departure of Miss Courtenay: this was Captain Powis, to whom her vivacity, and gentle consideration of his feelings had rendered his visit to Powis Court a scene of happiness. Her quick appreciation of his merits, and her unobtrusive, but constant endeavour to show him that they were prized by her, had made a deep impression on the mind of a reserved, and proud, but not insensible man; unaccustomed to society, and looking upon females in general as the most vain, frivolous, and ill-judging part of the species. He saw her enter the high-built, yellow, clean-looking chariot, which Mr. Cattell hauled out about twice a year, with a pang for which he could not account. " She is but a girl," he said to himself, " and by the time that I see her again, she will be spoiled enough no doubt. Such

men as Sir Charles will soon destroy the simplicity of a young girl's mind. It is obvious that
at present she dislikes him: yes, her heart is
happy in its unconsciousness of any preference.
I wish her well, and should fate ever bestow
prosperity upon me, might perhaps wish her to
feel a dearer interest in me." Thus parleyed
one, who was seldom known to " commune"
with any thoughts but his own.

Constance, as she entered Newberry, thought
it looked duller and more formal than ever.
There is something peculiarly chilling to young
and ardent minds in the regularity and monotony of unintellectual retirement. The hope-
lessness of change or interest, the absence of
all prospect for to-morrow, save a repetition of
to-day, are felt at an age when it is in the order
of things that the state of the mind, as well as
of that of the body, should be progressive.
Constance felt her heart sicken within her, as she
saw Mrs. Cattell resume her position by the fire-
place, and Mr. Cattell his place in the arm-chair,
and thought, that to a daily recurrence of all
their dulness, and drowsiness, she was condemned for the approaching winter. She almost

looked with aversion upon the little tea-tray, the formal, slender, well polished candlesticks, and all the insignia of a set-in, long evening. But she had too much sweetness of disposition to repine, and too much wisdom to complain of what was inevitable; so she resolved to make sources of amusement for herself.

In the first place, after a long night of un-disturbed rest, she determined to acquire the valuable habit of rising early, and walking be-fore breakfast, a resolution not difficult to put in practice after nine hours' sleep. She dressed her-self quickly, and hastened out into the street, se-cure of meeting no one that she knew, at that hour, and sanguine in her hopes of enjoyment of a clear autumnal morning's walk. The quiet little borough might at all times well challenge the inquiry, whether its inhabitants were all at church, once made by a traveller passing through one of our county towns, in the middle of a summer's day. As Constance moved briskly along the clean, but unaccommodating pavement, constructed before the use of flag-ged stones in streets occurred to the mind of man, she discerned not a living being, except

the parish clerk, returning from ringing the six
o'clock bell, and an old decrepit woman, who
was seated upon the steps before a door, apparently much fatigued. Constance passed her,
not without some compassion, as she contrasted
the worn-out appearance of the woman with her
own light-footed pace. She walked through the
town, and entered upon a large meadow, commonly known by the name of Lammas Land,
from the circumstance of the hay upon it, not
being allowed to be mown until Lammas-tide;
for this piece of ground appertained by some
old charter to the town of Newberry, aud its
produce was one of those many perquisites to
the corporation, at which the reformists of that
ancient borough were greatly scandalized. Passing along a narrow path, our young and agile
heroine seated herself upon a stile, from which,
shaded by clustering branches of hawthorn, in
berry, and overhung by a natural canopy of white
briony and nightshade, she could view the
grey towers of the churches, and the old-fashioned gable ends of the town, not yet emerged
from the morning mists, though partially irra-
diated by the god of day. A faint hum of hu-

man sounds, broke, but dispelled not, the tranquillity of the scene, which was enlivened and
ruralized by the lark's matin lay, and by the
distant sheep-bells, tinkling along the adjacent
common.

I shall perhaps be laughed at when I say,
that I do not believe there is any habit calculated to form the character of the young, more
beneficial than solitary walking. Thrown upon
its own resources, the mind inevitably becomes
imaginative, or reflective : the excess of the
former is, it is true, an evil ; but is soon modified
by the pleasures of society, and the cares of life ;
whilst the latter renders us independent beings,
for none can truly be reckoned so, who cannot
bear the necessity of thought. The train of
Constance's meditations was, however, disturbed
on this occasion by the approach of the same old
woman, that she had seen in the High Street
of Newberry. She dragged a weary pace, her arm
laden with a basket, and the bright red cloak
on her shoulders seeming to oppress her feeble
form with its weight. As she drew near the
stile, Constance descended from it, saying to her,
" Good woman, let me help you with your basket."

" Thank you, young lady. "

" How far have you to go? I will carry it a little way for you."

" Nay, 'tis not for such as you to carry an old woman's basket; but if you will,—I live at Bird-brook, close again the trees yonder."

" O, I can walk there !" said Constance, stoutly proceeding with the basket on her arm, but acknowledging to herself that she found it very heavy.

" And what have you been to Newberry for, good woman—to fetch these eggs?

" Nay, not wholly that," said the old woman, with a sigh—" I went to fetch a letter, and found none. "

" And was it from one of your children? and were you much disappointed ?"

" Ay ! but it's not the first disappointment that I have had in my day.   Two fine boys have I lost; one at sea, the other got a kick in training Sir Charles's fine hunter, and he never held up his head afterwards.   They say he broke a vessel —but he was long on the bed of affliction, but now he's at rest, yonder in the churchyard."

" And have you no daughters, good woman ?"

" None, thank God ! sons are enough for a poor lone widow; one indeed I had, but she lies by her brother. She went to live in service with a relation of Sir Charles Marchmont's in London, and came home to me in a consumption, and of that, not all the doctors in the world could cure her."

" I hope that Sir Charles was kind to you upon that occasion," said Constance, hesitatingly.

" He was but a boy of fifteen, then," said the old woman, " and knew nothing about us, but he would give the coat off his back to any poor soul that wanted help. When he came to the Priory after his tour, two years ago, Mr. Bouverie made it a point to tell him how that my poor Susan caught her death in his relation's service, and since that he has been very good to me—too good—too generous for his means, poor young man !"

" And is he, then, in embarrassments ?" asked Constance.

" Why, my good Miss, they say that every inch of his estates is what they call mort-

gaged, and he has not wherewithal to keep up
his rank, poor young gentleman !" As she thus
spoke, they came to the last stile, which separated the highly cultivated field, along the edge
of which they had been walking, from a rushy,
three-cornered slip of ground immediately adjacent to the village church : here they parted ; the
old woman with difficulty gaining the narrow,
but distinct path which led to her home, through
the churchyard, and Constance bidding her farewell, after receiving instructions how to find her
out when opportunity offered. With a light
step, and a countenance glowing with health
and good-humour, she retraced her steps, and
reached her guardian's abode, fortunate enough
to enter the breakfast parlour, before the last
spoonful of Bohea had been inserted into the
little silver tea-pot.

The monotony of Constance's existence was
such, that she soon found the love of news and
of gossip, which pervaded the town of Newberry, becoming infectious. Soon after her return thither, the universal theme of conversation was the close attention, not which Sir
Charles Marchmont was paying to Mrs. De

Courcy, but which Mrs. De Courcy was paying to Sir Charles Marchmont. Miss Pearson counted the number of times that her pony carriage was seen to drive down the High Street, at a certain time in the day, when Sir Charles was frequently known to return from hunting: the mild, but spiteful Mrs. Crawfurd observed that the young widow had become very blooming of late, her colour being, as Lady Teazle would say, " fresh put on:" whilst even Miss Monckton, whom Constance usually deemed above the gossip of the place, remarked, that it was strange Mrs. De Courcy should change her seat at church, the one which she had recently chosen, being just opposite to that of Sir Charles. In short, the ladies made common cause against her: so decided is their indignation, when they conceive one of their sex to be encroaching upon the privileges of the other, namely, that of making the first advances ; or suspect her of disgracing her own feminine nature by being won, unsought. In proportion as their resentment against Mrs. De Courcy was excited, their watchful interest in Sir Charles's conduct was aroused. Miss Pearson cross-examined his servants, intrigued with his tradespeople, and never lost sight of his minutest proceedings. Miss Monckton rallied him obliquely, sneered when Mrs. De Courcy's name was mentioned, and could scarcely keep her temper on the subject. Mrs. Crawfurd made skilful in- uendoes, saying to Mrs. De Courcy severe things with a sweet smile, and covering the sting of her speeches with a flattering sua- vity of manner which looked like real regard. Mr. Bouverie seemed incredulous, and dis- missed all their insinuations with contempt. Mrs. Cattell had made up her mind that Sir Charles would never marry a person of such " inferior family as Mrs. De Courcy's, whose fa- ther was an attorney;" whilst Constance wonder- ed at herself for being inquisitive and disturbed upon the subject, and found herself looking out of the window much more frequently than formerly. Affairs were in this state, when Sir Charles fell dangerously ill; a fever, caught in some imprudence in hunting, and in the excesses of society, not then wholly redeemed from occa- sional intemperance, threatened for some time his existence. All Newberry was inconsolable, for he was no less admired, than beloved. Every one had some kind, and liberal action of his, to relate, some virtue to extol, some loss to lament. Mr. Bouverie never left his sick room, nor could Sir Charles have a better friend to counsel him, either in the ways of life, or in the valley of the shadow of death. To this excellent man, of whom it might be truly said, in the fine language of Cowley, that he had " the light, without the fire of youth," other descriptive lines of the highest panegyric by the same poet might also be with justice applied. All prose must be feeble, when compared with language clothed in such verse as this:—

His mirth was the pure spirits of various wit,
Yet never did his friends or God forget;
And, when deep talk and wisdom came in view,
Retir'd, and gave to them their due.
　For the rich help of books he always took,
Though his own searching mind before,
Was so with notions written o'er,
　As if wise Nature had made that her book.

But even Mr. Bouverie's philosophy seemed at times cast down by fears, lest his friend should be cut off in the prime of youth, and, as per-haps in his secret soul, he might think, ere yet his character had received the true impression

of a living faith. He avoided all company,
however, and spoke but little on a subject,
which notwithstanding all his fortitude, agitated him not a little. But whilst all were
grieved, Mrs. De Courcy's distress was outrage-
ously afflicting ; and it was that sort of sorrow
which the least acute could not help observing.
Instead of her usually spirited demeanour, she
drove her beautiful poneys with a listless air as
if she cared not whether they took her into
the next ditch or not. She sent three times
a-day to the Lodge, to inquire, *sub rosa*, how
the young Baronet was : she was twice carried
out of church fainting, and wore no rouge
for a fortnight. Of course, as Miss Monckton
observed, if Sir Charles recovered, he would be
obliged to marry her from gratitude. At
length, after an illness which had nearly bowed
his young frame to the dust, Sir Charles was
pronounced convalescent. The physician and
apothecary, who had shaken their heads as
they dealt their cards at the evening parties,
began each to claim the honour of his cure.

"I can assure you, madam," said Mr.
Doubledose to old Mrs. Ruding, "I never

found my line of practice to fail in those cases. People talk of nature, and a fine constitution, medicine is superior to both. Medicine constitutes a second nature. Really, madam, men need never die of common diseases now-a-days: though I don't believe that there are five people in England who know how to prescribe."

Thanks to nature, and a fine constitution, however, and in spite of the regular attempts made to murder him in a regular way, by the united blunders, prejudices, and misconceptions of Dr. Stately and Mr. Doubledose, Sir Charles's recovery was as rapid as that of a young man of twenty-five, who really wishes to be well, and endures, rather than desires sympathy, usually is. One fine day it was rumoured that he was seen leaning on Bouverie's arm, on the bridge: the next, he drove out in a new phaeton, ordered, as soon as he could write a line, from London. In a week or two he was able to dine at Lord Vallefort's, a distant relation, and very soon afterwards, to mingle a little in the usual society of the town: for Sir Charles, well born and highly bred as he was, had one good principle which would have well become a better man. He accommodated, without lowering himself to his neighbourhood, and excited no ill-feelings which, by a little courtesy, he could avoid creating. Such was his popularity at this era, that poor as he was, had he offered himself as member for the borough, there was no doubt, as Miss Pearson from calculation affirmed, but that he would have succeeded.

CHAPTER VIII.

Their days insipid, dull, an' tasteless,
Their nights unquiet, lang, an' restless;
An' even their sports, their balls, an' races,
Their galloping through public places.
There's sic parade, sic pomp, an' art,
That joy can scarcely reach the heart,

BURNS.

CONSTANCE had soon an opportunity of seeing how great a chance there was of Sir Charles being spoiled. All the *elite* of Newberry went to the autumnal races at the county town at a few miles distance. Of course the old family chariot was moved out, looking like a large edition of those little tin carriages which one sees in toy shops, and reinforced with four post horses, the fat humoured beasts which composed Mr. Cattell's stud, not being permitted to undergo the fatigue of a long day's sport. Without,

was Thomas with a large nosegay in his button-
hole, and aside him Mrs. Mitten, her hair arranged in four flat curls, a close border of good
lace round her brow, a black pinched-up bonnet,
most mysteriously fastened on without strings,
concealing her face, in which there was a great
show of hypocritical gravity, whilst a vast deal
of pleasure rioted in her heart.   In the interior
were Mrs. Cattell and Miss Monckton, Mr.
Cattell declining, preferring, as he said, " To
ride a race with his own grey mare," though,
by the pace, it must have been a race with a
snail.   Between her two protectresses sat Constance, looking like a rose-bud between two
Michaelmas daisies, and converting, by the
mere gaiety of her heart, every little incident on the way into a source of merriment; for
to the light-hearted, there is scarcely any subject from which amusement may not be extracted.   The road was, as usual on such occasions, thronged by every sort of conveyance,
from the neat chariot and four, or the stately
family coach, to the little chaise-cart, looking as if it were going to shake out its contents
of men, women, and children, at every instant.

When Mrs. Cattell and her party reached the race-ground, they entered the stand, and Constance was enabled to enter fully into all the. dull routine of a day of pleasure.

The room and balcony were filled, but chiefly with ladies, for the gentlemen being, or endeavouring to be thought, learned in turf matters, preferred remaining on horseback or in carriages. Hence, on entering, Constance perceived only two specimens of the male sex, to relieve the eye amid a succession of pink ribbons, and gowns of that pure white with which London belles are seldom acquainted. Occupying a tolerably large angle, sat the five Miss Tribes, whose brothers, James and Edward. were the only beaux who set an example of brotherly attention, or of a gallant preference to the fair sex ; but envious report, in the person of Miss Monckton, assigned as a reason, that Tom could never be taught to ride, and that Edward was loath to soil his new white buckskins : insinuations at once frivolous and spiteful. Not far from the five sisters, but seemingly insensible of their presence, sat the pretty Mrs. De Courcy, fondling in her arms one of the diminutive dogs which bear King Charles's name, and which seem to have been born to afford a suitable accompaniment to beauty and affectation. The dress of the young widow was studied in the extreme, yet so perfectly adapted to her form and face, that one might conjecture the little Sylphs and Gnomes, who presided over Belinda's toilet, to have regulated hers. The Miss Tribes, all spick and span new, in new lilac spencers, new Leghorn bonnets, new white worked gowns, new yellow gloves, new dust-coloured shoes, with their redolent faces beaming with the effect of fresh air and hearty appetites, their thick-set figures, with that seeming uncompressibility which country stays give, presented, each severally, and all collectively, as striking a contrast to this lady, as a daub affords to a well-finished picture. Whilst Constance could not but pity the absorbed yet anxious countenance of the widow, she envied not the perfect contentment of the Tribe family, there was something so totally unspiritual in their joy. To be dressed, to be on a race ground, with beaux and horses in perspective, seemed to be their sum of human happiness; their minds appeared to comprehend the present tense only: the past and the future were alike forgotten. Unluckily for Constance, she found herself instantly entrapped within the vortex of their stupidity. They seized upon her, by right, as a young friend, concluding that she must be delighted to get to them from her Duennas. Mr. Thomas Tribe grinned from ear to ear as he placed her between the insipid Miss Dora, and the deep-voiced, brown-faced Miss Hester. James, the man of figure, strutted before in all the dignity of five feet four, a height to which none of his family, father and mother inclusive, had attained. Then they talked to her of themselves and their brothers, as of the subjects most interesting to her and to every one. Constance thought that anecdotes of the Tribe family would never end. They had cousins innumerable, their aunts and uncles were interminable, and all had a degree of Tribe-like importance attached to them. Things went on in this way for some time, when a slight bustle near the door announced a fresh arrival, and a stiff, proud-looking man entered, conducting, as by right, to the very centre of the front seat, a

pale, genteel-looking girl, whose plain but
costly dress, high carriage, and chilling manner,
announced an aristocratic importance. Her
features had been arranged by nature with symmetry, and were stamped by sense and reflection,
but wanted the sweetness of an affectionate disposition, and the vivacity of a happy mind. She
looked on the gay scene passionless, and without enjoyment, and took not the slightest notice
of those around her. This party was soon announced to Constance, from the diligent inquiries of Mr. Tom, who ascertained it to be
Lord Vallefort, and his daughter Miss Herbert:
he farther declared the young lady to be the
first-cousin of Sir Charles Marchmont, an
heiress, and related, both by her maternal
and paternal kindred, to some of the first
families in England. The entrance of these
grandees was quickly followed by that of Sir
Charles, who appeared to belong to their party.
He lingered, however, before joining them, nor
betrayed any of that little pride which some-
time induces weak people to slight those beneath them when higher powers are present,
but greeted his Newberry friends with his usual

gaiety and urbanity. He was stopped in his progress to Miss Monckton and Mrs. Cattell, by a supplicating look from Mrs. De Courcy, from whose dark eyes the most brilliant glances emanated upon his entrance, and even her dog Flush was thrown into agitation by the wished approach. The face of the young widow glowed with a hue so bright and natural, and her delight seemed so genuine, that the Baronet must have been more than man had he not devoted some moments to her. All eyes, at least those of the Newberry people, were directed towards them, and by many, the long-nourished conjecture was resolved into a conclusion, that Mrs. De Courcy would become Lady Marchmont; but whether the fair widow were herself of that persuasion was not so obvious: it only appeared evident that she wished it. At length, released from so agreeable an interruption, Sir Charles with a smile and a bow, moved onwards. He was again, not unwillingly, entrapped within the net of Tribes, who had within their power a victim of no small interest; for Constance, somewhat pale from lack of amusement, and weariness of those with whom accident had thrown

her, seemed to him even more attractive than
when in the full indulgence of her natural spirits. His intention of speaking to her was however frustrated, for he was still in the trammels
of a course of interrogatories from the elder
Miss Tribes concerning a race which had just
been run, when another entrance summoned him
to fresh duties.

The door was thrown wide open in a manner
expressive of coming events, and Sir Robert and
Lady Dartmore were announced by the whispers of the beholders. Her ladyship's entrance
seemed to electrify the " natives," as she herself
called them, for nothing so resplendent had
been as yet seen that day. As a taste for bio-
graphy is natural to the human mind, a few remarks upon her ladyship's early history may
not be deemed impertinent. She was the natural
daughter of a peer, who had pensioned off a
lady with three daughters, enabling her, as a
compensation for the charms of iniquitous splen-
dour, to assume a factitious respectability.
Hence, the once comely Mrs. Stevens passed as
an officer's widow, and finally, by her extremely
discreet behaviour, succeeded in becoming the

wife of an attorney in a country town   Years
passed away, the daughters grew up in loveliness and plenty, and their mother blessed the
limb of the law with scions of his own.   His
happiness, and her propriety, were the themes of
universal remark among the " gnatlings," as
Pope calls them, in that confined region, a country town, where observation, being pent within
narrow bounds, is proportionably eager.   A
fresh subject of self-exultation presented itself
to the happy husband, when he was told that
a certain nobleman, a distant relation of his
wife's, intended to honour him with a visit.
All due preparations were made, the lovely
daughters were presented to their kinsman in all
their attractions, when to the consternation of
their father-in-law, he claimed them for his
own, and establishing that claim by indisput-
able proof, announced his intention of introducing them to the world as such.   Retrospection was vain, and the prospect of some professional pickings through "my lord's" influence, and the hope of assistance to his younger
children, induced the polite lawyer to hush up
the matter.

Transplanted from comparative obscurity, the three young ladies and their brother, of whom Lady Dartmore was the eldest, soon felt the disadvantages of their equivocal origin. The great and high looked askance upon them— with the middle classes they had no longer any thing to do The charms of the eldest sister were ripened into maturity before a suitable offer of marriage occurred. It was at a county ball that Sir Robert Dartmore saw, and paid her some attentions. On the ensuing day, her brother, a notorious shot, waited upon the Baronet, and offered him the lady or a pistol. The Baronet had scarcely recovered from his astonishment to find that his gallantries were taken in so serious point of view, before the marriage preliminaries were settled.

They married, and for some years Lady Dartmore shone in the hemisphere of fashion with a brilliancy which was not, in the early days of their union, eclipsed by her birth, or diminished by some parts of her character. After a short career of gratified vanity, however, mortifications began to arise. She had set out by proclaiming an insolent indifference to the stigma upon her origin; this, in a young beauty, was admired by the men as high-mindedness, and thought clever by the ladies, as a piece of policy. By degrees it disgusted, was accounted indelicate, and became, in the eyes of the world, effrontery. She declared at first, that she knew herself to be the handsomest woman in London, and that she would never disguise from others that she thought herself so. This also did very well at first, but when her beauty began to wane, it was expected, but in vain, that she would leave off saying so. People will not be driven into believing that which they can see to be an error. They were tired of her ladyship's face, and would not be brow-beaten into saying that they were not. Added to this, certain unblushing indiscretions began to make prudent people shy of her. The men were afraid of one who would shrink at no public display of her conquests. The women are always sure to be clearsighted on these matters.

Sir Robert and Lady Dartmore took refuge in the country, and here after the first brush of initiatory dinners, they also began to feel that the world loved them not. And now shone

forth Sir Robert's characteristics. In London,
board wages, busy tradespeople, non-communi-
cation between acquaintance in small matters,
and the practicability of returning, or not, the
visits which you pay, or of being out of town
when convenient, all combine to cover the de-
monstrations of parsimony. But in the country, one cannot get off so easily. Sir Robert
was a man who, in the possession of five and the
expectation of eight thousand a-year, narrowed
to the very narrowest his expenditure. Obliged
by dexterous management to settle three hun-
dred a-year upon his wife for pin money, he
made up for that gulf of expense by every
possible deduction from the compound addition
which accumulated upon his hands. To enter
into the details of unnecessary parsimony, is re-
volting. Suffice it to say, when in town, he
bargained for inferior meat, kindly took off the
fishmonger's hands fish which he could not
dispose off, bought his liveries in Holborn, gave
out soap, candles, coals and potatoes himself,
and kept with difficulty, for few would remain
with him, just half the number of servants
which any other person in his station would

have maintained. In all points except expense, he was hen-peeked to a degree by his consort; but where money was concerned, he was inexorable. She rated, she ridiculed, she deafened him with her attacks, but she could never extract one single additional shilling from his purse. Yet Sir Robert, with this grand defect, had some respectable points about him. He loved study, and was that most useless article of all literary lumber, a fine classic. Allow him a tallow candle, and a Greek lexicon, and he troubled no one. By many, he was despised for the latitude he allowed his lady wife, but the confidence he placed in her was the only generous part of his nature. He knew that she despised him, and that she was vain even to the verge of licentiousness, but he believed her incapable of sacrificing her honour, if that can be called honour which, whilst it is acknowledged to exist, is totally severed from purity of mind. He thought that her attachment for her children would prevent her bringing degradation upon herself, and he was right; for Lady Dartmore had for her offspring that sort of fondness which coarse minds feel, something of the

nature of brutish tenderness, alternately beating
and caressing, but little resembling that intense, yet chastened love, which a gentle and
sensible female experiences for her children.
But we will close this long digression, and return to the Race Stand.

" What a regular *canaille*!" said Lady
Dartmore, as she entered the room, and advanced, as by right, to the very best seat, dis-
placing all who were foolish enough to be inti-
midated into that act of submission. " There's
not a well-dressed woman in the room," she
continued, a little raising her voice, as if she were
saying something which would give general satisfaction ; and turning round to her husband,
who crept in behind her, looking as if his
clothes had been made for him six years before, with an air of abstracted no-meaning on
his countenance, " Sir Robert," she almost
thundered, " desire the people to open those
windows at the side there, for I'm suffocated
with heat."

Sir Robert obeyed her, but having more proper feelings than his wife, moved along with a
supplicating look to the motley assemblage, who

were put into commotion by this command.
His operation produced a revolution among
some of the company, for Mrs. Cattell and Miss
Monckton took instant flight from the threatened danger, and Constance, not sorry of an excuse to leave the Tribe family, prepared to accompany them. Sir Charles, whose natural po-
liteness was struggling with his impatience,
stepped forward to conduct her to her friends.
He managed also to say in a low voice,
" Miss Courtenay, if you go to the ball to-
night, may I have the honour of dancing with
you the first set?" when Lady Dartmore, per-
ceiving him, shouted out, " Sir Charles Marchmont, I have reserved a seat for you by me."

As she turned to speak, Constance thought
she had never seen any face which conveyed so
complete an idea of perfect beauty, but it was
the symmetry of beauty only, its expression was
absent. The dark and flashing eyes, full opened, and clear as in infancy, when the distinction
between the pupil and the white of the eyes is
most strongly marked, the pencilled eye-brow,
the forehead, and nose, chiselled, as it were, by

the hand of nature with exquisite delicacy, the faultless mouth, and the profuse and shining hair, might well establish for Lady Dartmore the reputation which she loved best, that of a beauty. But here her charms ceased: an unskilful substitution of artificial for natural colour, gave to her countenance that mask-like look by comparison with which the triumph of nature's hues is most obviously shown. Her expression was fierce, voluptuous, and inflexible. There was no repose in her features—nothing to dwell upon, no melting variations; the fire that kindled in her eyes was that of passion, not of genius. Sir Charles hesitated complying with her summons, until Constance, withdrawing her arm from his, assured him that she should not go the race ball, and sat down between her elderly friends. She was not so far, however, from Lady Dartmore, as not to overhear, although reluctantly, some of their conversation.

" My dear Marchmont," said her ladyship, " think of my distress. You know Dartmore Park was full of visitors last week—I wanted them all to stay the races—but one after another disappeared. Never, as I could take my oath before a court of justice, did any woman behave better to these people than I did—but they all went, except poor Colonel Earle. Well, he too came the other morning to me, and said he had re-ceived letters from Scotland, and that he too must go. ' That's impossible,' said I, ' for the post has not been in this morning.' So he was obliged to own that it was all an excuse. So I would have the reason out of him, and what do you think it was? You can guess, I am sure."

" No," said Sir Charles, afraid of touching upon dangerous ground if he did.

" Well then, I will tell you"—glancing round to see if Sir Robert was very close—" He said, if he must tell the truth, that Sir Robert was so very little conversant with the duties of hospitality, was so silent, and so—so disagreea-ble I suppose he meant—that he could not stay. But I gave him the best reply in the world. ' Good heavens!' said I, ' you have no con-sideration for me — if it is so very irksome to you to be with him, who, I must own, is a learned fool, for a short time, what must it be

to me, who have his society constantly ?' So. I
had the best of it there, had I not ?"

"Certainly, your ladyship's reply was very
pointed," said Sir Charles.

"Tell me, dear soul," said Lady Dartmore, "the names and genealogies of some of
the people here. Absolutely their looks re-
mind me of a story of my dear Lady Lifford.
She was at a country ball, somewhere, and met
her wine merchant face to face at the door—
well, she behaved suitably to her rank and character, and declaring to the stewards, that the
room smelt so abominably of wine and spirits
that she could not abide it, left the company.
Tell me the names of the red-faced girls you
were talking to—don't give me a regular list—
it would be like a catalogue of monsters in a
museum, for I never saw such fresh-caught divinities in my life; they looked as if they had milk-
ed their fathers' cows, and churned his butter.
Their dress is of the year one. And are those
animalculæ you were talking to their brothers ?"

"A very worthy family," said Sir Charles,
" to whose kindness and hospitality——"

" Yes, I should think they would *feed* people well; both their guests, their cattle, and themselves."

" A very needful duty, nevertheless," said Sir Charles, somewhat slily.

" O yes! well, we'll leave them alone, sweet little cabbage rose-buds! you can't marry them all, so you're safe there. Sir Charles, you must introduce me to your cousin—you hesitate— you sad hypocrite, you're afraid of my finding out your secret—are the settlements begun?"

Constance, she knew not why, hung almost breathless to hear Sir Charles's answer.

" That, my lady, is a question, which ladies may think themselves privileged to ask, but which a gentleman is equally privileged to refuse answering." His colour rose as he spoke.

" Well, I won't vex the dear little soul by impertinent inquiries. Is she called handsome? I don't think her so? she looks like a piece of orange-blossom, with that white face, and green dress."

" Her complexion is, at least, *natural*," said Sir Charles, emphatically.

" So you really defend her, and pretend to marry her for love. I know she's as proud as

Lucifer, and I can't endure pride. I never was intended to be born in a high station, I've so little pride myself. Had I been a village girl I should have been more thankful ; I am sure it would have suited me much better than the best station. What do you think ?"

" I make a point of agreeing with a lady ;" replied Sir Charles, with a suavity which made it impossible for Lady Dartmore to take his reply in bad part.

Thus ended all that Constance heard of their conversation, for Mrs. Cattell, true to her dinner hour, summoned her to the carriage, and Constance, not without a little of the heartache, left the scene which had just become interesting to her, in obedience to the commands of her chaperon. She had not even the gratification of a bow from Sir Charles, who, occupied with some strangers, was unconscious of her departure.

" How can I," thought Constance, " expect him to look at or think of me, engaged and flattered as he is by the great and the gay? How foolish I was to suppose that he even recollected my indifference and rudeness to him on the night when he saved me from drowning? Why should I cherish such intense gratitude to one who feels no interest in me? It is true, my gratitude is due to him, but he would have performed the same acts of kindness to Miss Monckton or to Mrs. Cattell, or to others, had they happened to fall in the way. I have, in my own mind at least, paid him the full tribute of thanks for his services to me. I will now endeavour to think of him no more." Thus she reasoned with herself, and, to the beloved inmates of a numerous and happy family, there may seem little difficulty in the performance of her resolution. But Constance, destitute of those ties which interest others, had in her character a depth of feeling, impassioned yet pure, which wanted some object upon which to expand its tenderness. To imagine that any one regarded her with interest, was not, as to the habitually beloved, a part of her daily portion in life; but a source of joy, amounting almost to rapture. To the generality of my readers, this assertion may seem exaggerated: by those who have been situated like Constance, it will not be discredited. The fond and anxious looks of parental love, the rapturous caress of a mother, prepare us for the expectation of those dear ties, which Providence in mercy has allotted to sweeten life, and render us even fastidious in our notions of what ought to be felt towards us. But these Constance had never known. The love bestowed upon her, by those whom her life had hitherto been spent, had been directed by duty; the attentions she had received had been paid for;—disinterested and involuntary attachment was at present new to her; and in all, but especially in the young, there is a quick discernment of the difference between real fondness and general benevolence

CHAPTER IX.

Then merrily, merrily went their Tabors,
And merrily went their toes.
See Scott's Demonol

CONSTANCE replied with a dispirited a.
Miss Monckton's inquiries of " how she
enjoyed herself." These inquiries were
in a gloomy, stately, untouched, untr
sleeping room, in the house of a
of Mrs. Cattell's, where they where to din
remain all night. No prospect had been
out to Constance of her going to the Rac.
Miss Monckton would have taken her, h
not like to go without a gentleman.
mily they dined with were lon~
minuet dancing. Constance had
her plans for a dull evening, thank
for Miss Monckton's company, for

looks of parental love, the rapturous embrace of a mother, prepare us for the expectation of those dear ties, which Providence in mercy has allotted to sweeten life, and render us even fastidious in our notions of what *ought* to be felt towards us. But these Constance had never known. The love bestowed upon her, by those with whom her life had hitherto been spent, had been directed by duty; the attentions she had received had been paid for:—disinterested and involuntary attachment was at present new to her; and in all, but especially in the young, there is a quick discernment of the difference between real fondness and general benevolence.

CHAPTER IX.

Then merrily, merrily went their Tabors,
And merrily went their toes.

See Scott's Demonology.

CONSTANCE replied with a dispirited air to Miss Monckton's inquiries of " how she had enjoyed herself." These inquiries were made in a gloomy, stately, untouched, untrodden, sleeping room, in the house of a friend of Mrs. Cattell's, where they where to dine, and remain all night. No prospect had been held out to Constance of her going to the Race ball. Miss Monckton would have taken her, but did not like to go without a gentleman. The family they dined with were long past even minuet dancing. Constance had therefore laid her plans for a dull evening, thankful, however, for Miss Monckton's company, for there was

a spirit both of ill-nature and benevolence in
that lady's conversation, which amused her.
She was not, therefore, thinking of the ball,
when she declared herself to have been disappointed in the races. Just then came that important arrival, a note, sealed with a very large
coat of arms, and directed with as much precision as if it had been going to the Indies.

" My dear Miss Monckton, what do you
think it is ?" said Constance.

" What ?"

" Why it is an invitation to go to the
ball to-night with Mrs. Powis, but she has
not asked you ; you must go with us:—I will
not leave you in this dull place by yourself.
Where is Mrs. Powis, that I may go and ex-
plain to her that you are here ?"

" But of this Miss Monckton would not hear ;
so Constance was obliged seemingly to acquiesce,
and to put in a little sly postscript which she
hoped would procure her friend an invitation.
She was disappointed, for Mrs. Powis, though
good-natured herself, was under the control of
her son, who was afraid that his horses would be
fatigued by going the length of one street twice,

as the carriage must have done, had Miss Monckton made their party five instead of four. A merciless silence on the subject was therefore agreed on, which puzzled Constance not a little, as she felt reluctant that her friend should know of that inattention, and yet fancied that it might be intended as an assent. This circumstance greatly lessened the pleasure which she felt in her preparations for her first public ball, but her friend manifested unmingled satisfaction in assisting her, and in inspecting her toilet.

Punctually at eight o'clock the carriage, with Mrs. Powis's compliments, stopped at the door, and Constance, not without much chagrin at leaving Miss Monckton, was quickly conveyed to the scene of gaiety. The race-ball of a country town was then, as it is now, frequently held in the county hall, boarded over, and adapted to its change of purpose. Thus, the rendezvous of judges, barristers, and attorneys, at an assize, and the arena of provincial orators at a public meeting, became the theatre where beauties made their *debût*, and beaux their conquests. Race-balls have been, from time immemorial, the concentration of all that is gay and splendid in the districts where they are held. Here country mothers formerly first introduced their daughters to the pleasures of that world, of which they have heard the rumour only in their nurseries, " at a safe distance, where the dying sounds" of fashion or of folly,

Fall like a murmur upon the uninjured ear;

or for which they have been holding preparation in their school-room and dancing academy. Unfledged youths, who had just learned how to ask a lady to drink wine at dinner, and who had but recently commenced the anxieties of wishing to please, were here first initiated into the knowledge of their own importance as elder, or inferiority as younger, sons. The high-born and the fashionable here enjoyed the full privileges of their distinction, their descent, property, and station in society, being here more thoroughly known than in the democratic haunts of contaminating London. A strong line of demarcation was drawn between the denizens of the town and the freeholders of the country; and this the exclusive country belle not unfrequently rendered more visible, by the conde-

scending manner in which she turned, or the
haughty manner with which she refused to turn
the burgesses in the mazes of a country dance.
The room, chalked with an incomprehensible
device, and lighted by dingy lustres, rendered
still more lugubrious by wreaths of laurel, was
but half filled when Constance, with her party,
entered. Those who had arrived were amazons
of the neighbourhood, noted for their assiduity
in the dance, and for their diligent search after
partners of a more permanent character than
those of the dance merely. There were the three
Miss Grantleys, famous each for tiring half-
a-dozen men down in an evening. There was so
much display of steps and attitudes about these
young ladies, and they had such an established
reputation as good dancers, that it was thought
an appropriate thing for young honourables, and
commoners in their teens, to come out at their
first ball as the partners of one or other of these
damsels, as it was sure to bring a young gentleman into notice; although it was observed
that the honour was rarely sought another
time. There stood the neat, quiet daughters of
some country clergyman, in bold relief with the

experienced votaries of fashion from some gay
watering-place, or perhaps the metropolis itself.
The gentlemen were a still more motley crew. In
most country places, except a detachment of military come to the rescue, there is no medium in
the ages of the beaux—they are either too young
to be of importance in society, or too elderly to
adorn it by their exterior. This, to a certain extent, was the case on this occasion ; and when
Constance first entered the ball-room, there was
every appearance of her being condemned to the
forlorn hope of figuring with a school-boy, or
of hobbling down with gentlemen who might be
her grandfather. But the entrance of a party of
modish-looking young men, in Miss Herbert's
train, dispelled these gloomy fears, and put
a whole row of young ladies into a commotion of pleasure. The most conspicuous
figure of this newly-arrived group was Miss
Herbert, considered by universal suffrage as
the principal personage of the room, and by no
means apparently herself opposed to that opinion. To dismiss this young lady in few words :
there was nothing to criticize about her as ill-
bred, inelegant, or disagreeable. To assume a

precedence, which by common consent was allotted to her, was not considered blameable ; yet
humility in one so young would doubtless have
been graceful, and even captivating. That which
has been said of her manners, might apply to
her face and figure. There was nothing objec-
tionable in either, except that the perfect quietude
of her countenance and the stately languor of her
movements, took from her the attributes of youth,
and scarcely left her one of its charms. Constance, as she gazed upon her unperceived,
thought it scarcely possible that the intellectual
Sir Charles Marchmont could select so unvarying
a companion to attend him in his path through
life. His young relative entered, indeed, leaning
upon his arm, and a perfect intimacy appeared
to subsist between them ; but it resembled
the intimacy of habit, rather than that of
love. Fortunately for Sir Charles's inclina-
tions, Miss Herbert was appropriated as the
partner of the principal steward of the ball, and
with him led off the dance. Sir Charles had
therefore considered himself at liberty to ask
Constance to be his first partner ; nor had he
given entire credit to her declaration that she

should not join the assembly, as he knew that young
ladies generally contrive to go where they please,
and especially when a dance is in question. It was
with delight that he saw her standing by the
side of her chaperon, beaming with youth, and
health, and animation, but overpowered with
confusion, as he thought, at his approach. The
fact was, that Constance had hardly expected
that he would have claimed an engagement to
which she had scarcely assented : willingly, however, would she have made the experiment, and
she was prepared to negative the request of Captain Powis that she would dance with him, when
the aspect of the Miss Tribes, with scarlet bodi-
ces, all alike, and huge scarlet flowers impartially
disposed in equal number on the head of each,
and a perspective view of James and Edward,
in clean white waistcoats, black small-clothes,
and all the insignia of regular ball dresses, im-
pelled her to the rash resolution of accepting the
gallant Captain's proposition. Her surprise, however, was extreme at his asking her to dance, for
he had not been known, within the memory of his
friends, to have conferred such a distinction on
any young lady; his services being usually neither

offered nor required, except in cases of a distress, when a run upon maiden aunts, good-natured matrons, or even active and wonderful grand-mothers, occasioned a general turn out of all the effective forces that could be mustered at Powis Court.

The fate of Constance was just decided, when Sir Charles, his eyes glistening with more than their wonted vivacity, and looking, even in the presence of several elegant men, the most ele-gant person in the room, advanced and offered his hand to lead her to the dance; but he was immediately superseded by Edmund, who, with a flushing cheek, and a manner un-usually excited, claimed Miss Courtenay as his partner. Sir Charles's disappointment com-pletely overcame a temper naturally somewhat hasty: he expostulated almost angrily, when Constance, vexed and almost tearful, entreated him as a favour to herself, to drop the contest. The request was instantly acceded to, for Sir Charles, punctilious as men of his rank and time were, about his rights and precedence, knew how to yield, when to oppose appeared to pain a favourite individual.

It seemed as if Captain Powis desired to emu-
late his example, for he instantly entreated Constance to intimate her wishes to him, and assured
her that they should be obeyed. " No, Captain
Powis," said she, " I have promised to dance
with you, and do not wish to release you from
your engagement to me. My promise to you,"
said she, turning to Sir Charles, " was conditional;
but if," she continued with some eagerness, " you
will give me an opportunity of explaining it all
to you, I am sure you will neither be angry with
me nor with Captain Powis."

This was no difficult boon to crave; and
Constance, when her probation with Captain
Powis was completed, found herself the far too
happy partner of Sir Charles. Who, as they pa-
raded the ball-room, in a little interval of preparation, which often occurred in those days
when ladies chose the tune and decided the figure,
who would not have said that they were destined
for each other ? Her youthful beauty, of which
those who knew her best thought least; the spirit,
grace, and intelligence, which were displayed
in her familiar discourse; the " eloquent blood"
speaking, as it were, in her cheeks ; the eye, im-

passioned, yet unspeakably soft and innocent;—
these, and a thousand undefinable attractions
which were brought into play by the gaiety of
the moment, might well authorize the admiration of a man her superior in station, and
show her worthy of being his choice. On
the other hand, the accomplished Sir Charles
was proverbially dangerous and fascinating
to the fair sex. The uniform deference which
he paid to them, his high tone of feeling,
and mode of acting on every point where
honour and generosity could be concerned, the
variety of his talents, his address in conversation, and, perhaps, even the very circumstances of his unfortunate history, rendered it the
universal opinion that few women could receive
his attentions with indifference. Yet, had the smiling object of his preference possessed, at that
moment, the power of probing every secret of
his heart, she would have recoiled with horror
at her own incipient feelings towards him ; nor,
had she possessed experience to analyze his principles, would she have returned from the ex-
amination the happy girl she that night was.

She found courage, on the first onset of their

conversation, to tell him the cause of her breach of promise to him. Sir Charles laughed so heartily at her simple horror of the Mr. Tribes, that she almost repented having brought her friends into ridicule. Yet, in the volatility of her young heart, she could not refrain from laughing also. This beginning broke the ice, as it were, of that coldness, which the girlish timidity of Constance, and the consciousness of Sir Charles, had established hitherto between them. For the first time, the Baronet saw her in her true colours. The originality of her character, its native humour, the wildness of her spirits when uncontrolled, the enthusiasm, yet delicacy of her feelings, broke upon him by degrees; for he possessed a quick discernment of excellence, and that which he had hitherto only imagined her to be, he found her actually to prove. Very difficult did this young couple find it to separate when the dance began, and to stand, like a regiment of soldiers, in two separate lines, gazing at each other whilst an insurmountable barrier of form was between them. But in the now despised country dance, there were innumerable opportunities of little significant attentions which are

wholly impracticable in the measured step of
a quadrille. To lead down the dance with the
partner whom you preferred, was sometimes
the prelude to an offer at the end of it; in
poussette, many kind words might be uttered,
and even the separation in hands-across was but
momentary. But now it is all a system of setting and rigardooning; the gentlemen and ladies seem afraid to touch one another; they
figure away as if they were in the presence of
their dancing-master, and resign a partner with
whom they can have no communication beyond
a few syllables, with the same composure as
they make a balancée. In the happy days of my
heroine, it was permitted also, for a lady, after
dancing down thirty or forty couple, to take a
little breathing time at the bottom of her set
with her partner; and here the interrupted converse of the dance was frequently renewed with
spirits accelerated, not jaded by the exhila-
rating exercise in which they each joined.

" Did you observe Lady Dartmore this morning, on the race-stand?" inquired Sir Charles,
as he seated himself by Miss Courtenay.

" Yes, I not-only saw, but heard her."

" And what did you think of her? did you subscribe to the general opinion of her matchless beauty?"

" I thought her beautiful, certainly—but I believe she is a friend of yours."

" An acquaintance, not a friend; pray do not hesitate to say what you really think of her."

At this instant the lady in question entered the room, displaying all the advantages which full dress is supposed to give. Her form, rounded by self-indulgence almost into corpulency, seemed disdainful of the stiff stays, and tight scanty dress, which it was then the fashion to wear, and impatient to burst the restraints it was compelled to assume. But, while clipped in below, it was unmercifully exposed above, and made due amends by its display of neck and shoulders, for the tyrannical compression of the waist. Hence, Lady Dartmore seemed rather to waddle than to walk along the room, whilst leaning on the arm of a jolly fox-hunting lord of the neighbourhood, and followed by her husband, creeping along, as if he were afraid of treading upon her heels, she made her way into the centre of the ball room. Her hair was encircled by a bandeau of diamonds, and the extensive region of her throat and shoulders profusely adorned with jewels. Yet, attired as she was, she wanted the genuine attributes of a lady, and even Sir Robert had more the appearance of original gentility than his splendid wife.

" I should like," said Sir Charles, as he carelessly returned Lady Dartmore's gracious bow, " I should like, Miss Courtenay, to know your opinion of her."

" Well then—but it is very wrong to speak upon such slight knowledge ; she seems to me to have beauty without attractions, pride without dignity, courage without ease, fluency without wit ; and, from all I have heard, wealth without enjoyment."

" Tolerably severe, but undoubtedly true. And what do you say to her charming helpmate ?"

Why, I pity and despise him too much, if all Miss Monckton tells me be true, to say any thing about him."

. " To pursue your mode of illustration," said Sir Charles, " I should observe, that Sir Robert

comprises within himself all the machinery necessary to compose animated nature, without a
spark of its ethereal essence.   He has learning
without sense, narrowness without prudence,
for a man who goes into extremes in any way,
cannot properly be said to have prudence ; and
to crown the whole, you never can tell whether
he be asleep or awake.   He is the only man
whom I ever saw sleep standing : look at him
now, are not his eyes shut ?"

"They are," replied Constance, "and to say
the truth, that argues his prudence, for surely
those lack-lustre orbs must be half put out with
the brilliancy of his lady.   She reminds me of
Mrs. Bland, or Mrs. Mountain, in an afterpiece
which I saw.   She seems painted for stage
effect : in a room, it amounts to daubing.   But
I blush for myself, and for you, at passing our
time so uncharitably, and never will I again be
betrayed into such wicked ill-nature."

"Believe me, you are wrong in terming it so.
To dwell upon the frailties of our friends, to
accuse them upon conjecture, or to set down
aught in malice against the humble and un-
offending, is ill-nature.   But to discriminate

shades of character so coarsely blazoned forth
as those of Sir Robert and Lady Dartmore, is
unavoidable; unless you mean to close your
eyes upon all moral distinction, and to view all
men and women in the mist with which what is
called charity would seek to envelope all the
frailties and foibles of mankind."

"But," said Constance, "we are all too apt to err
on the other side, and to draw forth frailty, rather
than to disclose merit. Besides, I can never consider it as a *necessary* point of duty, to point out
failings so obvious as those of Sir Robert and
Lady Dartmore."

" Who is severe now ?" asked Sir Charles,
smiling.

But Constance was not allowed time for a
rejoinder, Mr. Powis of Powis Court claiming
her as a partner, Sir Charles being summoned
to dance with Miss Herbert.

Constance was now doomed to experience the
force of contrast, between a companion in her
pleasurable recreations, animated, intelligent,
and devoted to herself, and one who was absorbed in the consciousness of his own importance, and in the antiquity and grandeur of Powis

Court. He stickled much about the set in which they were to dance. One had a gentleman farmer in it, another was mediocre, another was mixed ; to be at the extremity of the aristocratical dance, was more sufferable, than to stand at the top of an inferior set. Constance, as she passed, and repassed a fashionable groupe, assembled round Miss Herbert, who chose to stand leaning on the arm of her cousin instead of dancing, wished herself in the bottom of the Red Sea. Nor could she help hearing some observations upon herself and her partner, which abashed her, because they showed her that both were the objects of notice.

" Sir Charles, who is that fine girl, walking with a certain Mr. Slender of Powis Court, I think they call his place?" inquired a gentlemanly, self-assured, looking man, who was one of Lord Vallefort's party. You need tell me nothing about the man : my nephew knew him at college, he was the far-famed fellow-commoner of Oxford, who was annoyed by a mouse in his chambers, and went to a shop to buy a trap. He engaged to take the mouse-trap on trial, caught the mouse, and returned the trap next day to the vender, saying, "it would not do."

Happily for Constance, she heard nothing more than this anecdote, for a vacancy occurring in one of the sets, she and her partner were soon engaged in the mazes of the dance. Soon after this exhibition, Mrs. Powis retired, and Constance was conducted to the solid and quiet mansion, where she was to pass the night, every inhabitant of which was, at the time of her demanding admission, plunged into profound and enviable repose.

CHAPTER X.

Silence, and whatever approacheth it, weaves dreams of midnight secrecy into the brain.—STERNE.

Fame caught the notes with her brazen trumpet, and sounded them upon her house-top. In a word, not an old woman in the village, or five miles round, who did not understand.—STERNE.

THIS was perhaps the first night in the annals of Constance's brief existence, that she had ever failed to close her eyes for ten minutes, after laying her head upon the pillow. In general, no sooner had her blooming cheek pressed its allotted place of repose, than her spirits, undisturbed either by fear or grief, were hushed into that tranquillity, which health, a good conscience, and a heart at peace with others, usually impart. - On the evening of her first ball, her slumbers were, as might naturally be supposed, less propitious; often did she review every little event of the evening. She had appeared among the gay assemblage, unknown and insignificant; yet she could not but perceive that the attention of strangers, and the admiration of all, had been lavished upon her. She had seen Sir Charles Marchmont courted by the great and the gay, yet she had found herself incessantly the object of his observation at a distance, and of his devoted attentions when near him. She could not be insensible, that it was her own attractions that led to this result; yet, like all who are highly gifted in one peculiar way, she thought, with little pleasure, that it was her beauty that produced the charm, but longed for some more permanent and definite hold on the affections of others.

" How happy, thought she to herself, are those who have parents, or at least kind friends, to witness their first entrance into society! I envied even the Miss Tribes, the fond, proud, approving looks of their mother. For me, I have no claim upon the affection of any one here, and it is probably compassion on that account only, that induces Sir Charles to show me any attention." This idea a little abated the fever of her spirits, and cast, she knew not why, a dejection over her. After a few minutes of sadness, brighter thoughts occurred. " Well," thought she, " whatever be the source, I may cherish his kindness, and prize his partiality, as that of the only being, except perhaps Miss Monckton, who has hitherto shown me regard." With these soberizing affections, she fell asleep; her adventures of the evening, her little triumphs, her playful observations, unshared by that pleasant sympathy which young ladies know so well how to bestow reciprocally, and her recollections of all that had passed, deprived of half their zest by the absence of one, to whom, in the luxury of confidence, she could impart some of those feelings which had not, as yet, taken too deep a root to be revealed. This was a deprivation, but perhaps not a disadvantage, and Constance, in the later periods of her life, found ample reason to rejoice that she had not had the temptation of making a confidante in any friend younger than herself.

On the following day, Mrs Cattell and her companions returned to Newberry. It was a gloomy, half-rainy afternoon, when they reached the dismal abode in which our young and beautiful heroine was to pass the long succeeding winter. Let those who murmur at the noise and inconveniences of a numerous family, experience, as a corrective, the oppressive dullness of a life without object, devoid of all very interesting ties, or destitute of rational society, to compensate for that deficiency. Constance felt a chill creep over her, and had a foretaste of many a gloomy day, as she entered her own primitive bed-room, and saw the same broad-bottomed arm-chair, with its polished mahogany arms, the same white dimity curtains, the same well-guarded windows, with dark green canvas blinds, the same imperishable carpet, looking as if even fairy feet had never ventured to make inroads upon its antediluvian patterns. She sat for some moments disconsolate, but a short period of reflection showed her the impolicy of discontent, and she resolved to " wrestle with the enemy." " I can, at least, be a source of consolation to the afflicted," thought she ; and she resolved to walk over to Birdbrook on the ensuing day.

Constance had before attempted to see the aged

person, whom she had mét on the Common, and whose name she understood was Rose Dean; but had found, on arriving at her cottage, the door locked, and had learned from the neighbours, that the old woman was absent at a neighbouring village, on some little errand, or occupation. She resolved, therefore, to choose a different and a less busy hour for her visit, than she had hitherto done, and storing her work-bag with such things as she thought might be acceptable to Rose, she set forward, exhilarated by the thought of making herself acceptable to one human being at least, and reflecting at the same time, how very limited had hitherto been her opportunities of doing any good, and how inexperienced she was, as to the best mode of effecting it.

She set off in privacy, not even confiding to Miss Monckton the pleasure she took in these solitary walks; for there is a feeling of independence, and of importance, in a little mystery, very tempting to the young and adventurous; and besides, it was more than probable that her prudent friend might have discountenanced these expeditions, so unusual among the careful maidens and matrons of Newberry, who would have been

afraid of cows, or of damp feet, or of the tooth-
ache, or what was worse than all, of spoiling their
clothes in a long walk. Leaving Mrs. Cattell
therefore in a safe doze, after an early, but not
hasty dinner, and Mr. Cattell writing a letter,
an operation which was seldom achieved by him,
except at repeated sittings, Constance passed
hastily through the streets, and ascending the rising ground, soon felt herself raised above all the
sublunary concerns of Newberry. The morning
had been wet, but the brilliancy of the afternoon
was enhanced in its charms by the little difficulties of small swollen brooks, purling along by
the side of the paths, or intersecting their course;
and the derangement of the earth's surface,
was finely contrasted with the serenity of the
blue and cloudless sky. Constance passed on
with a light step, but an unusually pensive
heart, till she gained the old church, within
whose precincts, even at this prime hour of the
day, a repose reigned, which was unbroken,
save by the flight and noises of a few rooks
perching their dark bodies on the pinnacles of
the rustic edifice, or affixing themselves to its
grotesque fane. " All here is rest," thought

Constance, as she seated herself on one of the tombstones, the shadow of which checquered . the pathway, " yet who knows what an aggregate of human woes might be collected from the simple annals of those whose last memorial is preserved here." As this reflection passed across her mind, her eye caught the inscription upon the head-stone of a small green mound, tufted with the hare bell, " To the memory of Susan Dean, aged nineteen, daughter of John and Rose Dean, of this parish;" beneath these expressive words,

" Depart in peace, for thy sins are forgiven thee."

" Poor young creature !" thought Constance, " this is doubtless the daughter of whom old Rose spoke. What sins could she have committed, that the record of them should be emblazoned here? Surely, so early a doom is sent in mercy to preclude the mastery of bad passions over the pure emotions of a young and innocent heart." Such were her meditations, produced partly by the scene and partly by the chastened, not to say melancholy, state of her own feelings, which seemed almost like the forebodings of evil to come, weighing down her spirits with an undefinable, yet oppressive sensation of me-lancholy. Rousing herself from her reverie, Constance passed onwards, closing the wicket behind her, and walked towards the small strag-gling village, pausing for a few moments to gaze upon the lowly, yet picturesque parsonage, the garden of which, belted with a low fringe of laurels, joined the churchyard. The smooth turf before the house was interspersed with parterres, which in spring bloomed luxuriant in flowers, and, even at this lovely season, exhibited, amidst the gloom of autumn, like stars in the darkened firmament, occasional remains of floral beauties; for still, near the house, the China aster and the Crysanthemum mingled their staring blossoms with the red leaves on the Virginian creeper, or the redder berries of the pyracanthus on the walls.

Constance gazed upon this picture of peace, and pondered upon the ideas of comfort and seclu-sion which it presented—a scene which, although it is so familiar to the English eye, yet is acknow-ledged to be almost peculiar to this country.

" Surely," thought she, " there is something

hallowed in a parsonage, as well as in a church !
Who can look upon this simple dwelling without envy, if the minds of its inhabitants be con-
sonant to the serenity which characterizes it?
Here is a haven of rest for the aged, or a
sphere of hope, and piety, and utility, for the
young and active." She moved onwards with a
sigh, for some yearnings for a home, and that
home the abode of love and elegance, and the
scene of virtuous exertion, had already at times
taken possession of her heart. But it was as a
dream which she acknowledged to have little
semblance of probability, and she banished it
with a vigorous effort from her imagination ;
nor dared to picture to her waking thoughts the
beings with whom she could wish such a vision
realized. She walked quickly through the scattered and ruinous looking cottages which composed the village of Birdbrook, and to which
small, but well cultivated gardens, and over-
shadowing trees, alone imparted an air of cheerfulness. It was Saturday, and the cottagers
were mostly employed at this time of the afternoon in cleaning up their narrow domains, and
in arranging the little furniture which they pos-

sessed. Constance observed that Rose had finished her task, and was seated in her oaken arm-chair within the enclosure of her ample chimney. A wood fire, her tea-things arranged before her, and the neat appearance, and composed, though sad and abstracted look of the old woman, presented a picture which the lover of village scenes might not have disdained to paint, especially as the leading figure, with the strong light reflected upon her brow and features, was not unlike one of Girardot's favourite subjects.

" Well, Rose," said Constance, " I have walked all this way to bring you some tea and sugar, and I am glad to see you look so well: but I have not long to stay, for I have loitered a good deal in your churchyard, and the evenings close in soon now." She sat down nevertheless by the deep inclosure of the fire-place; and if charity had brought her to Rose's cottage, curiosity now prompted her to stay; for she found that the old woman had once been a kind of upper servant in the Marchmont family. Rose was superior to most of her class in education and ideas, and possessing a natural discrimination and acuteness which are the

result of experience. Constance found in her
observations the charm of accurate and minute
description, by which the simple narratives of
such chroniclers are sometimes rendered more
instructive than an elaborate and well-turned
description.

Some minutes were occupied in various inquiries about the village, its pastor, and its concerns; and Constance learned from Rose, that
the living of Birdbrook was in the presentation
of the Marchmont family, for some member of
which it was at present held by Mr. Bouverie,
until Sir Charles should have a son or relative,
upon whom it might be bestowed.

" When he *does* marry," said old Rose ex-
pressively; " but he seems to think little about
that. Nay, he says sometimes he should like to
live here himself. ' Rose,' says he, one day,
when he called to see me, ' what think you of
my turning parson and marrying—coming to
live in yonder crazy old house, for I see no better prospect before me.' "

" And what advice did you give him ?" asked
Constance, with a deep blush.

" Go into the army, go into the army, Sir

Charles, says I, for you are fit for nothing but to be shot at. He was a boy then, miss, scarce sixteen, and made free with every body, or I should not have been so free. But we all liked him, down to the lowest stable-boy in his grandfather's service. His poor mother doated upon him."

" Was she like him ?" inquired Constance, with suppressed interest.

" She was, and she was not—she was, in the wild look of her eye, and in that random, thoughtless way he has—she was not in her features, for there he favoured neither father nor mother. I was waiting upon Sir Philip, Sir Charles's father, when my lady went off with ·Mr. Ferguson.—Perhaps you never heard of that, miss ?"

" I have, I have; and how was it — tell me all about it," cried Constance, ˙with an eagerness and impetuosity which she could not conceal. " Was she guilty ?"

" I believe so in my heart," replied the old woman, solemnly, " for she never loved Sir Philip. She was once so gay and so fine, they called her the belle, and the toast of the county; and beautiful she was. And there was this Mr. Ferguson that would have had her, only her friends would not let her, for they were set upon her being the Baronet's lady."

" Poor creature !" said Constance. " So it was a marriage of persuasion ?"

" That was the talk of the servants, ma'am; I was there often in her mother's house, helping, on great occasions, and long at Sir Philip Marchmont's; and it was not till the marriage was all settled between her and Sir Philip, that they would allow her to see Ferguson."

" And did she, then ?"

" I well remember, among the other servants, looking in at the dancing: the assemblies were then held in Newberry ; but since Lady Marchmont went away, they have all been broken up. I had a friend, who let me into the music-gallery; and there was my lady dancing away with the white feathers in her hair, and her partner was Mr. Ferguson, and he was the handsomest man in the room, and she was the handsomest lady ; and we all said, that she was fitter for Ferguson than for Sir Philip. And then it was said to be all friendship between her and Ferguson, and

she was married next week to Sir Philip. And
a year after that, there was a sad piece of work
with Mr. Ferguson, and he went away abroad,
as they said;—and if he had never come back
again, it would have been quite as well."

" He did return then?" asked Constance,
mournfully.

" Yes, he came back again, or Sir Charles
wouldn't have been Sir Charles now. I can't
tell you the ins and :outs of it, miss; neither
durst I, for Sir Charles don't like it talked of,"
she added, lowering her voice. " But he did
come back, and it's said, that it was my lady's
doing, and that she wrote to him to come post-
haste from Scotland, whilst Sir Philip was in
France, to fetch her away—she was so tired of
being all alone in that there Priory—and Ferguson travelled night and day till he came."

· " And Sir Philip—where was he? How
did he receive the news?—Her son, too!—how
could she leave him!"

" Aye, miss! that was a heart-break to her,
no doubt. But there's some things, and that is
one of them—the love of another man beside
your husband, that changes the very nature of a

woman. She left the boy, miss, though she loved him dearly—he was at school then, or it was thought that she would have carried him away with her."

" Then he was not quite a child," inquired her auditor, with emotion.

" Just turned of seven, miss; for seven years had Sir Philip and my lady lived together, after Ferguson left England. But they were like cat and dog together: he was a harsh, passionate, jealous man, fond of cards and such like, and always in debt and danger; and when my lady went off, he was in France, or Italy, or somewhere."

" Then he came home again, to his son, I suppose? Did he not?"

" O yes! home indeed! But he wouldn't come nigh the Priory, and we were all sent off to Marchmont. I went one of the first, and I shall never forget his coming home; and Sir Charles had been sent for from school, thinking that would soften him."

" And did it not?" said Constance, her eyes filling with tears.

" Soften him! no; it affronted him still farther. Now Sir Philip never liked that boy, nor the boy never liked his father. Some said, indeed, that Sir Charles was more like to Ferguson than to his father, and would have had it that he was Ferguson's son—and there is no knowing."

" O shame! shame!" cried Constance indignantly, and rising from her seat; but she sat down again instantly, checked by the look of surprise which the old woman gave her.

" I do not say it was so, miss," rejoined Rose; " but I shall not to my dying day forget how Sir Philip thrust his son from him, as the child came into the parlour full of spirits at being sent for home, and ran up to his father, asking for his mama.—Poor little lad! he never forgot it, nor forgave it, it is my opinion. I took him into the housekeeper's room : at first he stormed and pouted, but we amused him with childish plays, and the like. Then he begged and begged to go to his mama, and thought she was at the Priory, and wondered he had not been sent for there to see her; and cried so piteously, and begged so hard, that we all cried too."

" Cruel, cruel mother !" said Constance, weeping ; " and did he forget it soon ?"

" At last one of the servants told him that his mother was gone away, and would never come back again ; and I suppose his childish mind picked up some sense of her disgrace, and that— and the child turned sullen, and would not play nor be sociable, but went by himself, and seem- ed to pine like for a time. But, child-like, he did, after a few days, forget her, and we never heard him mention her name again. Nay, Adam Spencer, that has attended upon Sir Charles ever since they were both boys—and Adam is a good deal older than Sir Charles— remembers that his young master, long after he seemed to have forgotten his mother, would hang his head when her name was mentioned, and slink out of the room into the grounds, or somewhere."

" I must go, I must go, Rose," exclaimed Con- stance, as, turning to the window, she perceived the shades of evening gathering around them ; and wishing to conceal her face from the obser- vation of the old woman, she turned to the door. " Good bye, Rose ;—yet tell me," she added, as she lingered on the step, " what became of Sir Philip ?"

" Did you never hear, miss ? May be, it's best not to tell you.—Aye! the country blamed him sorely about my lady, far more than they did my lady—they said he had misused and neglected her ; and many of his intimate friends would not come near him. So the judgment of God fell heavy upon him," proceeded the old woman, clasping her hands, " and he died very sudden, and it was thought from something he had taken."

Constance sighed heavily. " Another day when I come, you will perhaps tell me of your own troubles, Rose—your daughter."

" My daughter !—you saw her grave, then ?" replied the old woman. She paused for a few minutes, and, communicative as she had been upon the miseries of others, seemed averse to touch upon her own ; so difficult is it, where the heart has been deeply wounded, " to give sorrow words."

" Farewell, then, Rose !" said Constance, tying on her bonnet ; " I shall soon come again, when I hope to have much talk with you about former days." She was about to lay down some money, but hesitated, feeling a pain in making Rose's pleasure in seeing her an interested one. "Yet such is the nature of these people," thought she; "their necessities both render them mercenary, and furnish the best apology for such a disposition;" and hastily placing a guinea on the old woman's table, she hurried out of the cottage, and turned her steps homewards.

It was one of those clear wintry afternoons, late in November, when the daylight disappears suddenly. Constance was aware of this, and drawing her shawl closely around her, began her walk in good earnest. She would have stopped, and asked one of the villagers to have given her his protection; but that would have destroyed the enjoyment of her independence, in the slight danger of which there was a degree of romantic pleasure; and besides, she felt assured that she could reach home before tea-time. With a mind filled with melancholy reflections and regrets, of which one person was the chief object, she passed through the church-yard, and was soon at the extremity of the adjoining field, when a large spaniel, known to her as the favourite companion of Mr. Bouverie's rambles, leaped over the style which she was about to mount. She had scarcely time to collect her thoughts, and to resume her composure, when she encountered the clergyman, somewhat to her confusion, for she could not' help thinking that he would consider her solitary excursion, so late, as an act of imprudence, if not of impropriety. The meeting seemed, however, to produce so much pleasure, that the surprise of Mr. Bouverie was superseded by more delightful emotions.

" I am sure," he said, with his wonted delicacy, " that some office of kindness has taken you to Birdbrook this afternoon ; but it is growing late, certainly : this is a lonely road. I must insist upon your accepting my protection home, and trust that you will allow me to offer you my arm."

" How thankful I am," thought Constance, as she accepted Mr. Bouverie's proffered assistance, " that it is not Sir Charles whom I have met. I should have had the whole town of Newberry ringing with the intelligence to-morrow."

" How delightful these autumnal afternoons

are for walking," resumed Mr. Bouverie, after
short silence ; " I love this time of the year
and of the day. There is a degree of calmness
which is almost heavenly in this partial gloom,
and even that melancholy, which pervades the
leaflessness of nature, is agreeable to my peculiar
feelings."

Perhaps, prone to religious reflection,
as he always was, any aspect of nature would
at this moment, have charmed the young Vicar.

" I have been much interested," said Constance, " in talking to Rose." She paused, and
scruples, which she could not but deem needless,
and a confusion for which she had no satisfactory reason to give, prevented her from
touching upon the main subject of the discourse with Rose. " Do tell me," she said,
" what was the history of Rose's daughter ; I
fear it must be a very sad one. I did not like
to ask her about it."

" It is indeed ; but perhaps it will be as well,
that Rose should tell you the story herself,"
answered Mr. Bouverie, with a little embarrass-
ment.

" The wounds which her daughter's sad fate

occasioned, are now somewhat healed, and it will perhaps be a relief to her to impart it to one so sympathizing as yourself, Miss Courtenay."

" Sir Charles Marchmont has been very kind to this poor old woman, has he not?" asked Constance, who could, at this moment, think of no one but Sir Charles, and who desired earnestly to bring him up to the standard of excellence which the young and ardent ever wish their favourites to attain.

" Sir Charles is always liberal and kind-hearted, and in this instance, he has been extremely so," was Mr. Bouverie's reply. " But I have never had an opportunity of asking you, Miss Courtenay," he continued, quickly changing the subject, " how you like the retirement of Newberry, after the gaieties of the races? It is very natural that at your age, you should find a void, which, in the absence of important duties, is apt to sadden the mind, in a society so contracted as ours. I am afraid we have no agreeable young acquaintance for you at Newberry."

" Indeed !" said Constance, " I should not mind that, had I any object of interest; mere amusement is not essential to me; my own little Emily will be with me in another year, for some months at least, and then I shall have something that belongs to me. She is almost the only relation that I have."

She looked at Mr. Bouverie as she spoke, and fancied that he regarded her with a more intense interest, than she had reason to expect.

" Few," he said, " are similarly situated— few so destitute of all endearing ties."

" Ah !" said Constance, " the ministers of religion can teach us how to bear the loss of friends; but can you supply to those who have no claim upon the affections of others, the enjoyments which kindred alone can give? I fear it is not in us that the love of God should be all-sufficient to us."

" Providence," replied Mr. Bouverie, not in a monitory, but in a soothing tone, " assigns no lot to us, which we may not alleviate by some efforts of our own. To those whose minds are not engrossed by near and dear connexions, general benevolence ought, in a great measure, to supply the place of strong interests; indeed, in all circumstances, it is not only an auxiliary to hap-

piness, but to fortitude and patience. I have
ever observed, that the most benevolent, bear
afflictions best. Their philanthropy enables
them to feel an interest in the joys of others,
even when borne down by calamity themselves.
With regard to the love of God, I think that
sentiment mingles so naturally with all our best
affections, is so intimately connected with all
well-placed and well-regulated human attachments, that, in that sense, and manifesting itself
in that manner, to our comprehensions, it *may*
be said to be all-sufficient to us. But I am
giving you quite a sermon."

" O no," said Constance, " and if you were,
I should like it, for there is not a single sermon
I ever heard from you that is not treasured in
my memory."

She said this in perfect innocence of heart,
but was surprised to observe, that the countenance of her companion was suffused deeply as
she spoke.

" Well, since you encourage me to proceed,"
he said, after a short pause, " I wish to illustrate
my point, by observing, that, as we have not a
single blessing which the rightly disposed mind

does not refer to God ; so also, when our affections are bestowed on improper objects, or even
our time and attention given to them, how
averse are we to admit the recollection of that
supreme Being as the governor of the universe !
We pray not for such objects, we thank Him
not in prayer for them. This is a proof, by
contrast, of the close connexion which we hold
with Him, when we cherish the innocent objects
of love which He has assigned to us, and in
which we trace the evidence of His benevolence.
But indeed, Miss Courtenay, I shall tire you.
You have drawn me into a subject on which I
should be apt to expatiate too long, were I
not afraid of making it apparently a subject for
display.   I can, indeed, only talk of religion to
those whom I respect and love."

Constance longed to ask, whether he ever
spoke upon the subject to his friend, Sir Charles,
but not knowing how to introduce the question,
even in the most circuitous way, she was silent.

" It is upon this account," said Mr. Bouverie, " that I dislike religious parties, and
other meetings of that description, held by sincere, but injudicious Christians.   The sacred

subject, which is most dear to all right-minded people, becomes a theme of argument, and a pretext for display. If all the party be of one mind, the discussion flags, or is likely to be so dull, as to render the most valuable of all themes, wearisome. If not, it shocks, in my opinion, the delicacy of a pious mind to 'bandy words' on such a topic. Besides, as there must be persons of various characters assembled, the humble Christian must, I apprehend, be often disgusted by what is vulgarly called cant, in religious matters. But it is a matter of taste ; to my own taste, these sacred societies are obnoxious ; but I do not mean to condemn those who like them, and I believe, that eventually, to the highest, and the lowest classes, this fervour of religious enthusiasm, so prevalent among some of the most cultivated, will be beneficial."

"And why not to the middling classes?" inquired Constance.

"Because the highest and the lowest classes most resemble each other. Their reasoning powers are least cultivated, their passions the most strongly indulged : hence whatever is addressed to the imagination and the feelings, and to those only, will have most weight with the majority of both classes."

As upon this, and various other topics, they discoursed, they entered the town of Newberry, both, in their own minds, acknowledging that the walk had been too short. Had Constance been with Sir Charles Marchmont, she would have rejoiced that it was now dusk, for she felt certain that she was unperceived by any of the gossips usually stationary at their windows. But she was mistaken, for the scandalous propensities of Newberry were too well organized, for some scouts from the post of observation not to be upon the look-out for news.

CHAPTER XI.

Had we never loved so kindly,
Had we never loved so blindly ;
Never met, and never parted,
We had ne'er been broken-hearted."

BURNS.

ON the following day, as Constance was walking to church, she was drawn aside by Miss Monckton, who whispered to her,

" My dear, are you positively engaged to Bouverie ?"

".No, dear Miss Monckton ; what can you mean ?"

" Because the cousin of Miss Pearson's servant saw you walking with him over the Lammas meadow last evening."

" Well, my dear Miss Monckton, it was by accident that I met him ; and surely I may walk half a mile with so grave, and respectable, and quiet a person as Mr. Bouverie, without being taken to task, either by Miss Pearson, or by any one else. You would not have wished me to have turned round when I met him, and walked home a different way." As they spoke, they entered the aisle of St. Michael's, and the conversation dropped. Constance was on her way from church, when Miss Pearson and Mrs. De Courcy accosted her. The former was evidently the jackall, catering for food in the form of gossip for the latter, who, for private reasons, chose not to appear interested about Miss Courtenay's marriage with any body.

"How are you, Miss Courtenay, after your long walk last night? You were late; it was twenty minutes past five when you came home, I hear."

Constance could not help laughing; "I am sorry," said she, "that any ladies should trouble themselves to look at their watches on my account, for I am sure I did not think about the time; I only regretted that it passed so quickly, Miss Pearson."

"It is a charming walk to Birdbrook, I

don't wonder you were late," observed Mrs De Courcy wishing to creep into a little confidence. " Sir Charles has often told me, that I ought to walk there some afternoon, and he is very fond of the walk himself."

" Is he?" said Constance, " I never met him there."

" No!" said Miss Pearson, her broad face widening into a laugh, " it was very lucky you did not meet him last night, for he would have been the wrong man."

" But perhaps Miss Courtenay would have had no objection to that, either," said Mrs. De Courcy, slyly.

Constance was angry with herself for blushing at this insinuation, but disdaining any reply, she said to Miss Pearson, courageously, " I *had* a delightful walk with Mr. Bouverie, nor can I see why ladies should not enjoy the society of superior men, with the same innocence and impunity, as they do that of intelligent women. You are quite welcome to publish my opinions, in Newberry, Miss Pearson."

" O, not all," rejoined that lady, " only, we all want to know," casting a side glance

at Mrs. De Courcy, " when we are to congra-
tulate you."

" Never!" if you mean with regard to Mr.
Bouverie replied Constance, with the impatience of a person, who rejects a suggestion
disagreeable to her. " I admire him, I respect
him, I almost love him; but he neither suits
me, nor I him ; and having said this, I shall
treat this subject with the silence which it deserves ; and I am sure that Mr. Bouverie will
do so also," she added, as she curtseyed quickly,
and bade the ladies good morning.

To those who are conversant with country
towns, it will appear by no means remarkable, that this conversation should soon be
reported to Mr. Bouverie himself. It was,
in fact, cunningly related by Mrs. De Courcy
to Sir Charles, with the hope of eliciting some
opinion from the young Baronet as to the merits
of the fair lady in question, or to her chance of
becoming Mrs. Bouverie. But Sir Charles
knew how to conceal his own sentiments, and to
penetrate those of others. The intelligence of
Mrs. De Courcy was not, however, thrown away
upon him; for the first time, it occurred to

him that his friend's feelings might be somewhat interested in the beautiful Miss Courtenay, and he resolved to sound him shortly on the subject; and such is the weakness of human nature, and such, in particular, the weakness of man's nature, that the very suspicion served to enhance Miss Courtenay's attractions in his eyes, and to increase his anxiety to be the first object of her regard.

It was after a *tête-à-tête* dinner, in the dining-room of the Priory, that Sir Charles, after some general conversation, began the subject. They were neither of them addicted to wine; the dinner table had been pushed aside, and coffee placed on a smaller one near the fire, when Sir Charles said, with apparent carelessness, " So, Bouverie, you were walking the other evening with the belle of Newberry."

" Whom do you mean ?"

" I don't mean Miss Pearson nor Miss Monckton, nor any one of the three Miss Seagraves, nor even Mrs. De Courcy; I mean one who would bear away the belle any where, Miss Courtenay."

" Well, and what if I were fortunate enough

to walk with her? I know others who would have had no objection."

" Oh! but you don't know the sensation it has excited in the town. The three Miss Seagraves are jealous, Miss Pearson is positively spiteful, and Miss Monckton is piqued because she thinks nothing less than a Viscount fit for her pet, Miss Courtenay, who has superseded the lap-dog and the parrot, and half-a-dozen macaws, in Miss Monckton's affections."

" I am much obliged to you, Sir Charles; you are so kind as to allow me the jealousy of the plain and elderly ladies, that of the young and the pretty you keep to yourself," replied Mr. Bouverie.

" But to convince you, my good friend, that you have little chance with Miss Courtenay, she was taxed with encouraging your attentions, when her reply was, ' I admire, respect him, but he neither suits me, nor should I suit him.'—Upon my soul, he blushes!— Why, Bouverie, my dear fellow, I did not think it was so serious with you."

" You misunderstand me, Sir Charles," said Bouverie, gravely; " I cannot, with my present prospects, think of engaging the affections of any woman; and that which I know I ought not to do, I will not do, be the temptation what it may." He turned away as he spoke, and a shadow of anger or vexation, or of something like it, rested on his usually tranquil countenance.

Sir Charles seemed unaccountably affected by this reply. He coloured deeply, and it was not until after some minutes had elapsed that he again addressed his friend. But Mr. Bouverie was insensible to his confusion, and was leaning his head on the chimney-piece in deep thought. He started, when Sir Charles said—

" Bouverie, do you remember that we promised to go to one of the Newberry routs to-night? I know you hate such dumb-show meetings, and so do I, but I do not like to disappoint the old ladies:"—and so they walked forth.

The party which they joined was more than usually animated, for Mrs. Powis, her son, and brother-in-law, and Miss Sperling, were staying in Newberry, and had joined it. Constance was playing chess with Captain Powis when Sir Charles and Mr. Bouverie entered. It was remarked by Miss Pearson, that she lost her queen immediately afterwards : then went two bishops; and a castle surrendered.

" Good heavens, my dear Miss Courtenay !" said Miss Monckton, " what are you about ?" In a few minutes she was check-mated. She looked up, and saw that Sir Charles was standing by her. He was watching attentively for her recognition of Bouverie, and saw, not without secret pleasure, that although somewhat embarrassed, it was far less so than that which she gave to himself; but the quorum of ladies, sitting round the room on little settees, or stationed, with visages of apparent thought, at the card-tables, agreed that whilst Sir Charles evidently was only flirting with Miss Courtenay, Mr. Bouverie was dejected, and perhaps rejected. They instantly made common cause in his favour.

" It was so shameful in her, to encourage, and then refuse him. She might wait long before she would meet with such another. What he could see in her, was a marvel." And the younger Miss Pearson, who would have had no objection to be settled at the Vicarage, remarked, that Miss Courtenay's girlish attractions might blind him for a time, but would soon cease to charm him;" an observation which came with considerable weight from a lady in her thirty-first year. He left early, upon the plea of business; and Constance, too easily forgetting his departure, enjoyed one of those happy evenings which inspire subsequent regret, when time or change have deprived us of the objects which once constituted our happiness. She dared not task herself concerning her sentiments towards Sir Charles: she ventured not to consider what were his towards her. She felt within her a newly-awakened sentiment, an interest different to what she had ever before experienced; and though it required no prudent friend, no unlooked for event, no romantic incident, to reveal to her that it was a very strong and a very new interest to her; yet she ventured not to consider what must be its result, so far as her welfare or happiness were concerned.

It was soon obvious to her that her walks, her visits, her occupations, were anxiously watched by Sir Charles, and that wherever she walked or rode, he contrived to meet or overtake her. It was now approaching to Christmas, the weather was clear, frosty, and delightful for the young and active, and not cold enough to chill the pleasures of conversation. The few recreations of Constance consisted in a walk with Miss Monckton, or an evening occasionally passed in the contracted society of the place : 'but whether she and her friend strolled through the old Elm avenue which adorned the Priory Park, and which by ancient usage was a public path ; or whether they wound their way over the Castle Bridge ; or whether they took a safe and sheltered course along a path skirting some fields to a neighbouring village, the favourite promenade of the town's-people, they were sure either to meet Sir Charles returning from the hunt, full of health, and high spirits, on his superb horse, or he joined them, as he happened to be going their way, or he overtook them by accident, or sometimes he acknowledged to have followed them, having a song for Miss Courtenay, or a book for Miss Monckton, or upon some pretext or other, he always contrived to see them. Miss Monckton took this, at first, very quietly, for she thought it extremely natural that two such delightful young people should enjoy each other's society, and if they fell in love there was no great harm; and as there never was any thing but the utmost respect to her, and deferential attention to Constance, she did not deem it necessary to sound an alarm-bell for the safety of her friend's heart, thereby letting her know that it was in danger. There seemed indeed no obstacle to their future union but Miss Courtenay's extreme youth, and Sir Charles's present difficulties: the one, however, was an obstacle which every hour diminished; the other, time, and economy, and skilful management, might obviate. The incumbrances upon the estates would be gradually lightened, Lady Marchmont's death might be ascertained, the title to the Priory property made good, and that estate sold to great advantage. These expectations appeared to Miss Monckton well founded:—yet still Sir Charles spoke not his too evident wishes, nor ascertained by words those of Constance; and Miss Monckton began to feel an anxious, as well as a deep interest in the matter. Nor was this out of character, for it is often observed that old maids delight in watching a love affair, on the same principle, I suppose, that the light-hearted are fond of witnessing a tragedy.

Such was the state of things when Constance was invited to " dance out the old year, and dance in the new year," at Mr. Tribe's. For the first time since her residence at Newberry, she felt the utmost reluctance to quit it. Her whole soul seemed to be centered in the place, and she could now picture to herself no happiness without its walls; every street in it had charms for her, every walk, each dell of its picturesque vicinity, every turn of the road from the Priory Park to the Phillbrook water was associated with the image of Sir Charles Marchmont. Let those who blame her for thus abandoning her heart to a lover not declared, recollect that such precautions are for the wary and experienced. It has always appeared to me that the generous and confiding nature of youth will not wait for such declarations as are necessary to justify oneself gravely for the sin of loving too well; nor will it calculate how and when, and upon the faith of what asseverations, the tribute of a heart is to be rendered.

Constance was not, however, permitted to yield to those predilections which might induce her to decline a visit to the Tribe family ; for Mrs. Cattell, who had a high opinion of Mr. Thomas and his brother, and considered them, she said, as the two most gentlemanly young men next to Mr. Powis that she knew, recommended her to accept it, in terms much stronger than usual. The dancing party was to consist chiefly of the family, Mr. Tribe senior jocularly observing, that " he could make up one cotillion and a fiddler;" but Sir Robert and Lady Dartmore were to spend a few days in the house, and Mr. and Mrs. Cattell and Constance were particularly requested to stay a little time also. Accordingly, on a bitterly cold day, the twenty-ninth of December, the old yellow chariot was rubbed up, the two fat horses put into harness, and Constance, with her guardian and his wife, conveyed to the residence of the Tribes. It was a large, rickety, banging and slamming sort of house, famous for breezes, in which there was a perpetual contest between the wind without, and the children within, which should create the greatest noise. Not one of the Tribe family

was ever known to shut a door without sundry
reproaches and entreaties, although Mrs. Tribe
was screaming out all day to Hetty, " Come
back ; you've left the door open.—Amy ! here !"
—"Well, mama."—"Shut the door, James, you
really have no mercy on us," &c. And Mr. Tribe
never sat down to dinner without saying to his
foot-boy, yclept, from courtesy, ' our man,'
" Benjamin, really my legs are perished ; no
wonder I have the gout—there's that outer hall
door open as if we kept an inn or a post-office.
There's not a servant in my house ever shuts a
door, Mrs. Cattell." All this admonition, which
only made one feel the colder, was thrown away
upon this large disorderly family, who might be
said to live extempore, and, from the unfortunate
circumstance of having a very good-tempered,
easy mother, one of the most grievous calamities
that can befal so numerous a household, were
always in confusion. The servants of course.had
imbibed largely the latitudinarian system : ringing the bell was hopeless under five or six repe-
titions ; mending the fires equally hopeless : they
were generally let so low, that nothing but the
utmost skill could recover them ; when, lo ! in

came a dusty house-maid in curl papers, and discharged a whole coal-scuttle upon them. Let those smile who live in tropical climates, but these are no small grievances in merry, but cold England. Yet nothing could spoil the tempers of the Miss Tribes: they laughed as loud when the fire went out as when it blazed; they made a regular joke of the bell never being answered, and seemed almost in a state of consternation when the servant happened to come at the first summons. One or other of the sisters was constantly on the search for the house keys, which were usually lost twice a-day, and one or other of their friends usually engaged in pinning up the gathers and closing the gaps in their gowns behind; for as fast as one separation was concealed, another came to view. With all this, their mirth was unabated.

" Do you not think, Miss Courtenay, my daughters have all very open countenances?" said Mrs. Tribe one day to Constance.

" If, for the term open, you supply the term vacant," thought Constance, " I can perfectly agree with you."

On the last day of the year, unusual prepara-

tion was, however, made for the reception of
Lady Dartmore, whose visit was considered a
great honour; for the Tribes were by no means
in the first set of county society, notwithstanding it was Mr. Tribe's frequent remark, that
he came of an ancient family—" the Tribes of
Israel."

Accordingly, as the servants said, a great
piece of work was made, and every thing was
put straight for once. Stair-carpets were cleaned
and beaten. Books were put upright that had
lain horizontally or obliquely for months; the
hammer of the carpenter, and the tools of the
glazier, were heard in all directions, and added to
the noise of the piano-forte tuner, and the additional banging of doors produced by the bustle,
made quite a concert.

Then the servants were to be tutored.

"Betty," said Miss Tribe, "you are not to
stick a piece of holly in the plum-pudding—it's
quite out now."

" A plum-pudding without a bit of Christ-
.mas in it! Why, it won't look noble, miss."

"No, I assure you, it's not used any where.
I am assured it's quite vulgar; and at Lady

Augusta's, the other day, we had only a little wine sauce."

" Little enough, I dare say, miss; for Lady Augusta 's not full-handed. Her housekeeping is no great shakes, Miss Tribe."

" Yes, Betty; but it's not fashionable to be full-handed now," said Miss Tribe, escaping from the kitchen, fleetly.

These, and similar hints, might be, it was hoped, available; but the difficulty was in tutoring the younger members of the ten Tribes, who, like the canary birds, were sure to be noisiest, when they were most wished to be quiet.

"Emmy, you're not to dance, even if you're asked; there 's not gentlemen enough for you. You're to sit down until you 're older. John, if Lady Dartmore or Lady Augusta, at dinner, should help you to anything, you should say, ' Thank you, my lady;' for instance, if you send your plate for potatoes, say ' Thank you, my lady.' "

" What should I say, ' Thank you' for," said John, who had not yet arrived at the age of civility—" they're not *her* potatoes."

" Fie, John," answered Miss Tribe, reprovingly ; but the younger branches of the family
applauded John's reasoning. " And O! I do
hope," said Miss Tribe, aside to Hetty, " that
papa will not tell any of his old stories—so
vulgar—I shall sink into the ground, if he
does."

" Nor quote Latin," said Hetty.

" Nor talk about the history of England,"
whispered Dora.

" Nor tell over again, that old story about
the loin of beef being knighted."

" Which we have had every Christmas-day,
since I began to dine in the parlour," said
Hetty.

" Lady Dartmore's sure to be pleased with
James and Tom," observed Miss Tribe. " Tom
is quite a flame of her's, she says."

" An abridgment of all that is pleasant in
man," cried Hetty, with a smile; " that is what
she calls him. She prefers short men."

" Perhaps James is rather too tall for her
taste," remarked Miss Tribe, with some elation
of spirit, feeling confident of her brothers ac-
quitting themselves well.

At length the heroine of the comedy, Lady Dartmore, arrived. Constance was in her own room reading, and indulging from time to time a few unbidden thoughts, when, by the confusion of tongues, the sounds of ineffectual bells, the unusual turbulence of the children, and the accents of Lady Dartmore's unmodulated voice, she concluded that the consummation of Mrs. and Miss Tribes' hopes was at hand.

In about an hour ·she was summoned into the drawing-room by the last dinner-bell, which was by no means, in this house, a certain symptom of dinner. The Miss Tribes, who were acting managers in their mother's household, had taken a great deal of trouble to assemble a select party for Lady Dartmore. There were, sitting in dismal silence on each side of the chimney-piece, Mrs. Powis and her niece, and opposite, Lady Augusta Tarell, an antiquated scion of a Ducal family, who had married her brother's tutor, now a clergyman of the neighbourhood. The beaux mustered were really respectable in point of number: first, there was Captain Edmund Powis, who, for reasons only known to himself, was again a visitor at Powis Court, whereas usually his visits were biennial only. Then appeared Mr. Powis, with his wrists enveloped in red worsted muffatees, to preserve those precious members from being frost bitten, and an air of extreme anxiety depicted on his countenance, whenever the door, as was its wont, stood open unnoticed. Miss Tribe had been determined to have some young men to amuse Lady Dartmore, who was avowedly indifferent to female society; but being quite tired, as she said, of Sir Charles Marchmont and Mr. Bouverie, or rather finding they were a degree above her, Miss Tribe resolved upon uniting two ends, namely, the gratification of Lady Dartmore, and the advantage of herself and sisters. The persons she had selected were these: first, Mr. Puzzleby, a young lawyer, expressly come from London to pass his short Christmas vacation with this worthy family; a keen, smart young man, second-rate, however, in talent, third-rate in person, and fourth, fifth, and sixth-rate in manners, conversation, and gentility. His own advancement in the profession was ever in his thoughts: be had a snare to litigation in every sentiment, a puff in every joke. Garrow, Erskine, Ellenborough, were constantly in his mouth—you would think that he ate his very dinner in the courts of law. His anecdotes had all travelled round Westminster Hall; his routes had all been circuitous; his details were all cases; his very hat was bought in Chancery-lane; his whole heart seemed at Nisi Prius. This gentleman had a pale, parchment-looking complexion, and one of those hatchet profiles which seem to be created purposely for lawyers : his very eyes had a legal near-sightedness about them; he spoke as if he were addressing a jury; he had the regular dusty look of a solicitor-general in embryo. Next in popularity to Mr. Puzzleby, was Mr. Saunders, an importation from a neighbouring county. This gentleman aimed at fashion; but he founded his claims on his having passed the last October and November in London, and concluding that every thing in the metropolis must be fashionable, splendid, and worth talking of, and having seen nothing but the fag end of things, he had come away,—poor young man !—in a lamentable state, worse than ignorance, of the relative importance of places,

people, and sights. He was a sort of man who
would begin by asking you " if you had been
to Astley's this season ?" and was in a wonder-
ment if you had not. As he is not worth much
description, we discuss him in these few words,
leaving the Miss Tribes to be in raptures about
his being so remarkably entertaining, and well
dressed—his new scarlet waistcoat, and his
" uncommonly gentlemanly" manners.

Constance had but just made her obeisance
to Mrs. Powis and Lady Augusta, and her
more distant curtesies to Captain Powis, whose
frequent gaze she had of late perceived and endeavoured to avoid, when the door was flung
wide open, and Lady Dartmore entered in full
sail. She came in the bustle of amber coloured satin, dressed far more than the occasion required, rouged far more than any occasion required, and making all the other ladies
look thin, pale, and shabby, especially Lady
Augusta, who was one of those grey looking,
drab-complexioned little women, whose rank
was not obvious in the cut of her gowns, nor the
adornment of her hair. All eyes turned on
Lady Dartmore, as she took her seat at the head

of the room, and gave a bold yet not penetrating stare around her; and Constance felt
her pride rebel against the peering glance which
she directed towards herself : but she was soon
deserted for more attractive objects, for Lady
Dartmore seldom took much notice of her own
sex, or if she did, it was to ridicule or scan-
dalize them. The beaux were duly presented
to her; first, Mr. Tom and Mr. James sim-
pered their compliments, Mr. Tom rising almost on tip-toes as he spoke to her. He hoped
her ladyship had found the roads good. " Execrable !" was her reply. Hoped she liked
———shire better than she did. " I detest it,"
was her answer. " Sir Robert seems pleased
with it," said James, with much humility. " Sir
Robert's taste and mine don't suit at all."

" Sir Robert," said she, with a voice which
roused him from his habitual reverie, " how
can you think of saying that you like ———shire
when you know I mean to go to Bath, and that
I hate your dull country quarters ?"

Sir Robert made some reply, but was in-
audible.

" Tell me who that ugly old frump is," said

Lady Dartmore, in a voice meant to be a whisper, but much more audible than that of her consort.

" Lady Augusta Tarell," said James, with great satisfaction.

" O, the Duke of what-d'ye-call-'em's daughter. Those people have been very rude to me; I can't endure them. So I suppose you mean to carry off that pretty Miss Courtenay, don't you, Mr. Tom?"

Constance could not avoid hearing this, and felt highly flattered, of course, at having her name coupled with that of so fascinating a hero. But she sustained it better than Captain Powis, who was sitting near Lady Dartmore, and whose face betrayed an emotion, first of surprize, and afterwards of indignation. His handsome and manly countenance, ever addicted to blushing, remained, indeed, suffused for some time.

" My brother," said James, " is an absolute Benedict."

" Indeed! then I am sorry for the young lady," said Lady Dartmore; but I fancy she can console herself elsewhere. Do bring her up to me—I want to know her; for if I give a ball, I shall perhaps ask her to Dartmore Park, if I like her on acquaintance."

Away went Mr. Thomas, but to his inexpressible astonishment he found Constance by no means disposed to accept the proffered honour, and by no means disposed to smile upon the charming Benedict.

Just then dinner was announced, and they all moved off for the dining-room, Lady Dartmore, with a very bad grace, being obliged to yield precedence to Lady Augusta Tarell.

"It were vain to tell," as they say in old chronicles, "what manner of meats, and subtleties with divers choices," were displayed in the repast which Mr. and Mrs. Tribe set before their guests. The party, excepting Constance and Captain Powis, were all of a description to be too much engrossed by their dinner to show off much of their natural character. Sir Robert and Lady Dartmore were famous for making up, at the houses of their friends, for the deficiencies in their own table at home. Lady Augusta, though she never appeared to profit from it, had the aristocratic faculty of eating

and drinking liberally.   The rest of the party
did very well, whilst Mr. Puzzleby contrived,
by way of *entremèt,* to slide into the good graces
of Lady Dartmore, who commenced a sort of
condescending flirtation with him, wheedled him
out of a law opinion, talked of her family
affairs, and told family anecdotes, until the rest
of the party were nearly sick of this all-engross-
ing beauty; and even the Miss Tribes gaped,
whilst Tom and James could scarcely keep up
their ever-flowing stock of good-humour.

But the most cruel blow was reserved for
Constance, when they returned to the drawing-
room.

" I must be introduced to this paragon, Miss
Courtenay," said Lady Dartmore, as she extended her capacious form on one of the broad,
high backed, commodious sofas, (now, alas!
out of vogue,) near the fire-place.

"O, I'm sure she will be so much honoured,"
said Miss Hetty Tribe. " Miss Courtenay,
allow me to take you to Lady Dartmore."

There was no retreating, and Constance had
scarcely time to curtesy, when Lady Dartmore

said—" I think you are acquainted with my friend, Sir Charles Marchmont."

" I do—I am," said Constance, her colour mounting to her face.

" Well, and what do you think of him; isn't he a dear, charming soul ?   He's very fond of me—I am a vast favourite, I assure you.   It is well Sir Robert is not jealous, as I often tell Sir Charles; but he laughs, and says if he were, he would be jealous of a great number.   What a pretty dress you have on, Miss Courtenay !"

" How am I to deal with such a character as this ?" thought Constance to herself. "She seems to think herself privileged to say any thing."

" Well, and so you do like my pet, do you ?" resumed Lady Dartmore; " and how long may you have known Sir Charles, Miss Courtenay ?"

" About a year, I believe."

" And did he ever tell you of his romantic engagement to his cousin? Good God, how surprised you look ! Betrothed to each other from the age of fifteen, I have heard; but he can't care about her—it's impossible. She is a piece of machinery, a *veritable* wax doll. She's monstrous proud, and has no heart.

But I suppose he *will* marry her, just for the sake of the dowry, and console himself with some pretty actress."

She paused, but Constance made no reply.

" You are quite shocked, I see, Miss Courtenay; but believe me, my dear, it's the way of all these men. But here comes Captain Powis, always first—ask him what he thinks of Sir Charles's morality? I heard him say one day, that if he had a sister, he would not trust her within twenty miles of him. But, good heavens! Miss Tribe—Miss Hetty—Miss Amy, bring salts, sal volatile; run to the medicine chest, Miss Courtenay's as white as a sheet."

" My——Miss Courtenay!" said Captain Powis, looking almost indignantly at Lady Dartmore, though he had not heard what she had said; " will you let me conduct you to the hall—this fire is overpowering;" and drawing her arm within his, he stalked out of the room with her, for she was too much overpowered to resist.

" Quick march! a military manœuvre," said Lady Dartmore, contemptuously; " I never heard of heat being overpowering on the 31st of December before."

She mused for a few moments, and rested her beautiful head on her hand.

" Well, I hope Sir Charles won't play Jerry Sneak any more; but, if he really prefers this Miss Courtenay to Miss Herbert, marry her outright."

This was partly addressed to old Mrs. Cattell, who sat in her usual state of afternoon inanity near the mischievous Lady Dartmore.

"Sir Charles! Miss Courtenay—I never heard —I never thought ; sure your ladyship must be mistaken; it is Mr. Bouverie that admires Miss Courtenay, my lady, I fancy; but I don't know."

" Bouverie! who is he?"

" Why he is a great friend of Sir Charles's ; —and Miss Monckton, or I should say Miss Pearson:—and my maid Mitten, thinks so too, that he would have Miss Courtenay if she'd have him."

" Sir Charles shall hear of this, thought Lady Dartmore to herself. This pretty young miss is not to run away with all the men; she may have Bouverie to herself: *faute de mieux,* I mean to amuse myself with Sir Charles."

" But your protégée's run off now with Captain Powis, ma'am," shouting so loud, that the
old lady, who was a little deaf, was quite affronted at Lady Dartmore's over zeal to make
her hear; for persons slightly afflicted in that
way, are remarkably ungrateful to those who
speak loud to them.

" O Captain Powis—she can't be with a
better person," she replied shortly.

" I dare say she thinks so herself, ma'am,"
rejoined Lady Dartmore, who never allowed
any one to have the last word.

Meantime, Miss Courtenay had recovered her
composure, and thanking her companion, begged
to be allowed to go to her own room. But
Captain Powis, for a shy man, was tolerably
pressing for her to remain a few minutes, lest
walking up stairs should overset her again.
His arm trembled as she leaned upon it, and
Constance, observing his earnest expression of
countenance as he looked at her, was suddenly
struck by a conviction of the nature of his sentiments towards her.

" I do indeed pity him," thought she, " for

he loves one, who loves another. Our fates are similar, but I will not act to him the ungenerous part, which that individual has acted to me."

" Will you not sit down in the library ?" said Captain Powis, " it will be quieter there ; I see that Lady Dartmore overpowers you."

" She does indeed," said Constance, and suffered herself to be led into the room.

" How can I undeceive him," thought she, " if he supposes his affection returned. O that I could spare him the misery of uncertainty, the agony of hopeless conviction ! But no ; fortunately for our sex, we are to be passive ; yet I will not lose the first moment that I can with propriety set him right."

She seated herself before a large blazing fire in the library, and unconsciously leaned her face in her hands. There were no candles in the room, and the light of this large, but ill-tenanted apartmant, fell upon the figures of Constance and her timid admirer, who stood leaning beside her, his eyes intently fixed upon the ground. A stranger, entering the room at that moment, would not be at a loss how to interpret their silence. To those who know not well the heart of man, it may seem strange that so reserved and diffident a person as Captain Powis, should venture to aspire to the favour of any woman at all, far less to that of one so admired, and so superior to those around her as Constance. But the shyest men are most determined in matters of love, and there is something dogged in their natures, which, when they have ventured to a certain point, prevents them from going back. Their perseverance is proverbial ; for they have in their characters a fund of vanity or pride, whilst it makes them jealous of exposing themselves to ridicule, sustains them when once the ice is broken. Captain Powis, in conjunction with an ample share of pride, possessed a great degree of sensibility, a generous and grateful heart. His interest in Constance had been first awakened by her gentle and delicate endeavours to prevent his feeling those slights to which she saw him daily exposed, by the insolent neglect of his relative, the squire. He had never felt the slightest approach to the tender passion before. His life had been past between fighting and sporting, and if he had ever experienced the least desire for domestic happiness, he had checked it as a wish, puerile, futile, and inconsistent with his profession. He was totally at a loss how to begin a declaration, and had often meditated in his own mind, in what way he should first plant his trenches, direct his fire, and persuade the fair fortress eventually to capitulate. From what he had read, and heard, he considered that offers were as formal as invitations: a solemn epistle beginning, " Since on you alone my happiness depends," or a set oration, commencing with a petition to be heard, and ending by a descent on one's knees, were, as he supposed, the legitimate modes of taking a plunge into the bay of matrimony, preparatory to reaching its haven. But now all his preconceived intentions put to flight, and his honest, manly feelings getting the better of him, he stood, his eyes fixed upon Miss Courtenay, with an expression, which had she seen, she could not have misunderstood. At length she raised her head, and recollected how strange an appearance their absence must have had. But, in her passage to the door, she was arrested by Edmund, who, for the first time in his life, ventured to seize hold of a lady's hand. She stopped, and raised her eyes to his.

" Is it not more honourable," thought she, "to put an end to all doubt, than to let him persist in hopes which may perhaps destroy his chance of settling in life for ever ?" Yet she felt the utmost agitation assail her, on being obliged, for the first time, to encounter the formal addresses of any man. Captain Powis did not leave her long in perplexity.

" Miss Courtenay," he said, gaining courage after he had passed the rubicon of those words, " before I saw you, I never felt the slightest preference for any woman, nor have I now a right, from any conduct of yours, to suppose, or hope, that you would ever condescend to think of me ; yet if you were so good as to give me hopes, you would find that the warmth of a soldier's love 'is only equalled by its constancy. I would give up any thing, even my profession," he continued, raising his voice, " if you could tell me that you are free, and that I may one day hope to gain your affections."

Constance had thought that she should feel relieved when she could explicitly undeceive Cap-

tain Powis on a point, of which she regretted
that she had not earlier thought more seriously,
and that she had not crushed his hopes in the
bud. But the earnestness of his manner, and
the novelty of the scene, to her, rendered her
reply more difficult than she had expected.
The refusal of a first offer, far from being a
triumph, is, to a generous mind, one of the most
painful incidents to which youth is liable. She
felt, however, that she had no time to lose,
and mustering all her energies, she resolved to
repay the candid avowal she had heard, at
least, honestly and decidedly. " Your request,
Captain Powis," she said, " is answered in very
few words: I cannot give you a higher proof of
the esteem and confidence which I shall ever
feel for you, than by my answer. I trust,
I am sure you will hold it sacred. Had I
known you sooner, I cannot say how I might
have felt towards you, but it is now too late."
Resolved to spare him the fruitless pain of a
reply, and overcome by a recurrence to her own
state of mind, she passed him quickly, and was
soon in her own apartment.

It was well for Constance that she had Cap-

tain Powis and his disappointment to engage
her attention, before dwelling. upon her own
thoughts. When she did recur to those, her
distress was the more poignant, that she was
angry with herself for the involuntary acknowledgment of her own attachment to Sir Charles,
which the Captain's avowal had drawn from her.

" Yet my love has not unsought been won,"
thought she. " How I used to' avoid, and almost dislike him ! Has he not often since com-
plained to me of my former avoidance? And
now, O Sir Charles ! were you but what you
seemed, you would not have to complain of my
coolness.—What will Miss Monckton think of
this?" again she reflected. " But no, I will
not, by seeking for sympathy, either lower
myself into an object of compassion, or reflect
dishonour upon him. I will subdue all my too
easily cherished regard for him, but my secret
shall die with me; for Edmund—the sincere,
generous Edmund—knows not to whom my
weak heart has been given. But what if that
bold woman should have invented this tale ?
Alas ! some such idea has been before suggested
to me, her discourse has only confirmed it. I

have been blinded by vanity, by ignorance of the world ; but it is not too late to tear away that veil—to withdraw my rash confidence."

Whilst thus ruminating, Constance was summoned down stairs ; and so retrievable was her happiness at this early period of her attachment to Sir Charles, that she felt she could, with some exertion, have feigned the semblance of a heart at ease. But a dread of again encountering Lady Dartmore's coarse raillery, and a fear of giving pain by her presence to Captain Powis, determined her not to return to the party, as previous indisposition afforded a fair excuse for remaining in her own room. We pass over the description of her solitary evening, her restless night, and the thousand resolutions which she made before morning, convinced that there is not a single young lady who has not experienced what we should necessarily describe. Her reveries, until she went to bed, were several times interrupted by the Miss Tribes, hot and breathless from the dance, with " O Miss Courtenay, we are so sorry you are not with us! Such a delightful evening, though we have not sufficient for the College

Hornpipe or the Boulanger,"—and by old Molly, the family nurse, who had spoiled and babyfied all the young Tribes, with a large bason of water gruel, and a dose of James's Powders, recommended by Mrs. Tribe, who thought that something must have disagreed with Miss Courtenay. At length, she was left to repose.

The following day happened to be Sunday, and Constance, in attending the simple village church, derived that consolation which never fails to accompany a heartfelt participation in our Liturgy, the compilers of which appear to have had every possible extremity, and every incidental want of human nature in their view, when they so admirably adapted our hebdo-madal petitions to the thankful, the powerful, the needy, and the afflicted. Constance left the sacred Edifice with a composure which was not entirely disturbed, even by the presence of Captain Powis, who, to her surprize, remained at Mr. Tribe's, and even accompanied the party to church, although he did not, as usual, offer Constance his arm. The freshness of a cold winter's day had given a bloom to her clear but varying complexion, and the consciousness of being more 'sinned against than sinning,' a contented, though pensive expression to her countenance, when, with Miss Hetty Tribe, she proposed walking along a sunny terrace, sheltered by one of those formal yew hedges which were the boast of our ancestors, who decreed that fated sepulchral tree to assume any shape but its own.

"Did you hear," said Miss Hetty, "that Sir Charles Marchmont has called here, on his way from Lord Vallefort's, and that he is walking with Lady Dartmore in the garden?"

"No, I did not know it."

"Lady Dartmore is only just dressed, for she never goes to church. Her piety, she says, is of the heart, and she can't endure formal observances, nor being bothered with long sermons."

"A dangerous description of her religious feelings, my dear Hetty; for doubtless these forms are necessary aids to our piety, which, without it, will, I fear, resemble a house without props."

"Gracious me!" said Hetty, "there are Sir

Charles and Lady Dartmore. How earnestly they are talking. Now I dare say it is all about papa, and mama, and us. I would give my eyes to hear what they say."

" Let us go back, dear Miss Tribe, for they are coming this way, and indeed I cannot see them now."

" You're in a vast hurry ; perhaps you prefer meeting Captain Powis," said Hetty, laughing. And so they returned to the house.

" You're a dear eccentric creature," said Lady Dartmore to Sir Charles, as they sauntered along the terrace. " Nothing surprises me more in you than your admiration of that pretty baby-flirt, Miss Courtenay. I verily believe, after all, you will jilt Miss Herbert, and marry this young lady."

" Your ladyship seems to have settled it so."

" Well, you'll have your choice; whether you like to fight that lean and slippered panta- loon, Lord Vallefort, or to exchange shots with that ramrod concern, Captain Edmund Powis, for each of these gentlemen will conceive them- selves aggrieved, let your choice fall where it may."

" Indèed! and what has Captain Powis to do with it—he is not Miss Courtenay's father?"

"No, certainly; but Captain Powis has a right to resent a lady's marrying another when she faints away in the young captain's arms, allows him to convey her into a library, and remains there with him an hour and three quarters, as I can testify from this dear little true monitor," said Lady Dartmore, placing her hand upon her watch.

" O, your ladyship's watch is apt to gallop sometimes," said Sir Charles, playfully.

" Well, you're incredulous—but I can refer you to a host of Tribes."

" Indeed, I have no right to interfere with Miss Courtenay's concerns," said Sir Charles, with some degree of irritation; " she may run off with Mr. Tom, and Mr. James, too, if she pleases."

" That's right—that's proper pride; and now I've a good mind to tell you what she said of *you*."

" Do; it will add to my satisfaction," replied the young Baronet, with an attempt at a smile.

" Why, she told me that she had, she

thought, known you about a year, but had seen very little of you, for truly she hated to be pestered with any man's admiration. And when I asked her whether she thought you were clever, the pert thing's answer was, Why, very well for a baronet, but it's well he's 'born to greatness,' for he'll never 'achieve any.'"

". Very gratifying; and the more so, as she seems to have taken the trouble of quoting from that old villain, Shakspeare, for the purpose of running me down."

" And had you heard how she said it. I long to see you together, and to observe with what infinite contempt you will treat her."

"That is not altogether so easy," thought Sir Charles to himself. " However, I will see what I can do."

" You'll stay here to-day to dinner, won't you, *mon ami?*" said Lady Dartmore to him, as they walked to the house, with one of her sweetest smiles. " Do; I'm literally *choaked* with these Tribes—their stupidity suffocates me. Then they're all so civil; absolutely they stick in the door-way. And then that James is so monotonous; his conversation falls unheeded

like a shower of rain, drop, drop, drop. And
only think of my being doomed to hear the history of all Mrs. Tribe's confinements, and Mr.
Tribe's improvement of the roads. But you're
quite in a reverie, Sir Charles. Well, I declare
this Tribe Hall is almost as bad as Dartmore
Park, with Sir Robert."

" I can hardly imagine any place dull with
Miss Courtenay in it, traitress though she be,"
thought Sir Charles, as he slowly drew his
heavy companion along with him up the ample
steps which led from the garden to the hall.
" Perhaps," he said aloud, " I may stay, for
the enjoyment of a little spiteful observation of
Miss Courtenay and Captain Powis."

" Do, that's a good soul, and I will assist you
in taking your retaliation. You shall see how
I'll show them up."

" Nay, Lady Dartmore," said Sir Charles,
making a full stop; " whatever Miss Courtenay
may choose to say of me, I will never be acces-
sary to the exposure of her imprudencies, or
the wounding of her feelings. Your ladyship
will act as you think proper; but if there is to
be any showing up, I shall run away, and per-

form my promise of dining with Bouverie. But
we have forgotten one important point—I may
not have an invitation to dine here."

"You will have at least a dozen," rejoined
Lady Dartmore, "reiterated from the seniors
of the family to Miss Matilda—though last, not
least. People like these are always hospitable."

"And can there be a better trait?" said Sir
Charles, as they entered a sort of low, long parlour, a kind of common room for the Tribe family, when they were at all on easy terms with
their guests.

CHAPTER XII.

" Ye blessed spirits,
Look down upon your daughter in her trouble,
For I am sick at heart."

WILSON—*City of the Plague.*

NEITHER Constance, nor her reputed admirer
Captain Powis, were in this apartment when
Sir Charles and Lady Dartmore entered it.

" I 'll lay my life," whispered she to Sir
Charles, "that they are closeted together in the
library."

She was mistaken; for, in a few minutes,
Miss Courtenay appeared alone. She was de-
sirous neither to seem to shun Sir Charles, nor
to behave as if she felt any resentment towards
him, nor to betray pique ; and yet she was too
ingenuous to demean herself towards him as

heretofore, although she was fully sensible of
the indelicacy of manifesting indignation for
the perfidy of a man, who had not made any
explicit declaration. Altogether, her situation
was very awkward ; but she possessed tact and
spirit to cope with it for a time, if her season of
probation happened to be short. The danger
was, that her strong and natural feelings would
get the better of her ; for Constance had none
of the propensity to finesse which is thought to
belong to the female character, but which is
often erroneously adopted by them in self-de-
fence. She had yet to acquire what is called
management of character. The necessities of
her present condition gave her, however, a lesson
in this art. Feeling what was due to herself,
she made a strong effort to return Sir Charles's
respectful bow with as little variation from her
usual manner as she could possibly effect ; she
was not, however, so successful, but that his
penetrating eye could mark a change—a smile
less fascinating, a glance less happy than usual ;
for, of late, the enjoyment which she innocently
felt in his society had been expressed when they
met, with all the artless warmth of a girl of

seventeen, and had, indeed, been met with far more than equal rapture on the part of the young Baronet. He now imputed the shade of coolness, obvious only to him, in her behaviour, to any thing but the right cause. "She is conscious," thought he, "of her real indifference to me; and I see clearly that she has allowed of my attentions only as a blind to those of a more favoured lover, though one whom her friends will not deem a good match for her. She has liked him from the first, and I have deceived myself."

This reflection stung him to the quick, for Sir Charles really loved Miss Courtenay, if that can be called love which had no perspective regard for her happiness or misery. Such as it was, it was heightened, although he would not acknowledge it, by pique, uncertainty, and jealousy; and instigated by these, he resolved in his own mind to take ample revenge upon the fair cause of his vexation. She, on the other hand, was considerably surprised at his change of manner, and it threw her out in her plan of action. For she could have found it easy, she thought, to retire from his usual attentions, and to shew him, without deviating from the gentleness of her sex, that they were no longer agreeable to her. But she knew not how to deal with a man who gave her no opportunity of repulsing him, and who made her look like the forsaken one. Besides, a young lady, much accustomed to attention, and from one particular person especially, is naturally depressed by neglect, and is awkward, not only from wounded vanity, but from being placed in a situation new to her. Those who have studied the feminine character, will acknowledge, that the young beauty, in the zenith of her career, has a far less need of strength of mind when receiving the incense that has become habitual to her, than when that incense is causelessly withdrawn, even if it be not offered to another.

Constance had, however, what is commonly called a good spirit. Unaccustomed to seek, or to receive advice, her dependence on herself had taught her to discriminate quickly, and to adopt courageously the part which her unassisted reason led her to think best. " I have no one to support or succour me," was her constant conviction. "Whom have in heaven but Thee, and I have none on earth that I desire in comparison of Thee?" were words which came home to her heart, in a peculiarly strong, and affecting sense.

In the present instance, she felt the conduct of Sir Charles to be the more unjustifiable, as he knew her to be unfriended, except by the old and almost imbecile persons whom the law called her guardians. Yet her indignation yielded to a bitter pang of disappointed affection, when the idea struck her that his changed manner was a confirmation of what Lady Dartmore had told her. Till then, she had cherished a faint hope—for love *will* hope, when reason would despair—that the intelligence might be false. Now she thought otherwise. "Lady Dartmore has told him that I know all, and he is now prepared to show me, by his altered manner, that he confirms her intelligence."

"Of course you will stay and dine with us," said Mr. Tribe to Sir Charles.

"O, of course you will," echoed Mrs. Tribe, or, as her husband called her, Mrs. T.;

" Of course you will," sounded from all the
Tribe family in succession. Of course, Sir
Charles was persuaded to do so. To Constance,
during the whole of a long and gloomy Sunday,
he showed a studied neglect; yet he had too
much good taste to evince his pique against her
by a well-acted flirtation with Lady Dartmore,
who would fain have enticed him to this species
of revenge, and who was only restrained by his
unflinching opposition to her schemes, from
making a complete party against Miss Courtenay.   As it was, she paid but little attention to
Constance, or indeed to any one except the
young Baronet, at whom she looked, with whom
she laughed and talked, until Miss Powis looked grave, and even Mrs. Cattell raised her head
from her celebrated soporific, " Hervey's Meditations," and gave a suspicious glance at the
fair manœuvrer.   Sir Charles was, however,
polite to all, and Constance, as she sometimes
raised her eyes from her book to look at him,
thought she had never seen him appear to so
much advantage.   The large party, who were
partaking of Mr. Tribe's hospitality, were
mostly constrained to remain in the house, and

formed little groups in various parts of the room. Mr. Puzzleby was expatiating to the elder Miss Tribe upon a case of breach of promise of marriage, which he had defended; Mr. Saunders was muttering soft unmeaning things to Miss Matilda. The consequence of both these gentlemen had sunk greatly since the appearance of Sir Charles; for Lady Dartmore had dismissed them entirely from her little coterie. She gaped at Mr. Puzzleby's stories, and gave a look of cold surprise when Mr. Saunders opened that narrow aperture in his face, called a mouth. As for Captain Powis, she could make nothing of him from the first; but to the young squire she was occasionally civil from the hopes of being invited to wile away some part of the winter months at Powis Court. At one period of the afternoon, she was endeavouring to hold Sir Charles engaged in one of those half whispers which she thought herself privileged to make. This he resisted, and persevered in maintaining a conversation audible enough for the rest of the company to join, if they pleased. These two occupied a sofa near the fire. On the settee opposite, wrapt in a thick

shawl, sat Lady Augusta Tarell, having beside
her her only child, who had come in the world
when Lady Augusta had ceased to be young,
or to expect such a blessing. Like a rose, blow-
ing in the autumn, this little plant was of
course an object of the utmost solicitude, and
a victim to all the tortures of over-tuition, over
dosing, and over-dressing ; she perched, rather
than sat, upon a little stool, with her feet in the
first position, holding in her stick-like little
fingers one of those good Sunday books
which are dull enough to make children hate
the name of the Sabbath. With this beloved
object Lady Augusta was far too much occupied to see, or think of any one else in the
room. Mrs. Cattell and Mrs. Powis were each
and severally in a large easy chair, looking as if
they had been created only to embody the essence
of dulness visibly to our faculties. Their mode
of rest was however different : Mrs. Cattell
was a lady of the poking description; her
head, despite her utmost endeavours to rouse
herself, nodded till it nearly touched the pious
work from which she had hoped to inhale some
Sunday virtue. Mrs. Powis, on the contrary,

having been an apt scholar in the ancient school of manners, was never known to bend her body forward for an instant: she even dozed in as upright a position as if her back-bone were made of cast iron. Her position was fixed, and the large Psalter on her knee stuck there as if it had been nailed.

At a Pembroke table near these venerable ladies, were assembled Mr. Tom, and Mr. James Tribe, Captain and Mr. Powis. This group had before them county maps, plans of new inclosures, newspapers, and Echard's History of England, with prints; for the days of Historical Memoirs, of Blackwood, and of the New Monthly, of the Age, and John Bull, were not then arrived. Of this party Mr. Powis was the most consequential, Mr. Tom and Mr. James the most loquacious, and the Captain the most abstracted. He appeared sometimes, indeed, to be listening to his kinsman's dissertations upon rabbit-warrens and ring fences, new roads and old roads, " my property, and my inclosures ;" at other times he seemed to be scanning the last gazetted promotions at the Horse Guards; but his eyes often rested with an ex-

pression of sorrowful reproach upon Constance,
who sat near the window reading, or endeavouring to read, one of the few books which Mr.
Tribe's library furnished. Captain Powis might
or might not be aware that the direction of his
glances was from time to time watched by Sir
Charles Marchmont, who, being seated with
his back to Constance, envied every look which
his rival gave in that quarter. But Constance
saw not, on this occasion, the gaze of her rejected admirer. She had, indeed, wondered at
his pertinaciously remaining not only in the
same house with her, but always as near to her
as he could : but she knew not the determined
character of the bashful soldier, nor was she
aware that he had guessed the object of her secret preference, and had resolved to stay, and
warn her against an indulgence of this early attachment. Perhaps, too, some degree of hope
still lingered in his bosom. At any rate, he was
resolved not to yield the object of contention to
Sir Charles Marchmont, without a struggle.

Time passed away heavily in this manner till
the half-hour dinner bell rung. At this signal,
Lady Dartmore was the only person who kept

her seat; and Constance, happy to be released, was, among the rest, hurrying to her own room, when Lady Augusta Tarell, who had all along shown her a marked attention, said to her,

" Miss Courtenay, my little Georgiana has taken such a fancy to you, that she wants to go with you, and to say her hymn to you."

Constance smiled, and extending her hand to the little girl, was about to take her out of the room, when Sir Charles, catching hold of the young treasure, said, " Come and say your lesson to me, Miss Tarell, you can't think what a much better instructor I shall make than Miss Courtenay."

" That you will," said Lady Dartmore, who had been longing all the day for an opportunity of affronting Constance, " for you won't teach her to secrete herself in a library with a young gentleman."

" The face of Constance was deeply crimson-ed at this attack, but it seemed as if her blushes were reflected on the countenance not only of Captain Powis, but of Sir Charles, who felt both indignant at the impertinence of this at-

tack, and vexed to see that it could not be re-
pelled.

"Well then," said little Miss Tarell, " as
you won't let me go, Sir Charles, and as you
still hold my hand, Miss Courtenay, you must
both come along together, and hear me say my
hymn in the little parlour."

And so saying, she attempted to pull Sir
Charles along.

" Lady Augusta, Miss Tarell is beginning
in good time, she's a match-maker already,"
cried Lady Dartmore, her rouge augmented by a
little natural passion.

" She does not show her discrimination," said
Sir Charles, trying to smile, but looking almost spiteful in the attempt, " for I am not the
happy man whose society in a separate room
would be selected by Miss Courtenay."

" I do not see," remarked Constance, whose
spirit rose at what she thought an insolent and
unjustifiable attack, " why my preference or
conduct should be an object of Sir Charles's ani-
madversion."

" Come now," said Lady Dartmore, who enjoyed this commencement of hostilities, " do let me see you two friends. You really appear to me to hate each other.—Sir Charles, I know you'll do any thing to oblige me ; do make it up with Miss Courtenay, who evidently owes you a grudge. But perhaps Captain Powis will act as mediator between you, for I am not intimate enough with Miss Courtenay to presume to dictate."

" There is no occasion, madam," replied Constance, with a grace and dignity which sprang from a guileless, but proud heart ; " I am quite unconscious how I have offended Sir Charles, and therefore cannot atone for an offence of which I am wholly ignorant."

" Dear me !" said little Miss Tarell, who was one of those hot-bed kind of children, who, from being a great deal with grown-up people, hear much more than they should do, " I wonder you and Sir Charles quarrel so, Miss Courtenay, for I heard my nurse say last night that she knew you were going to be married together."

" Georgiana—my dear Georgiana, I'm shocked at you," cried Lady Augusta.

" Well, but I don't wonder neither," said

the young tell-tale, wishing to atone for her re-mark, " that you and Sir Charles quarrel be-fore you're married; for I've heard papa and mama quarrel sometimes, and they are married, you know."

" Capital!" said Sir Charles, who could not help enjoying the confusion of Constance, " you're quite a little moralist, Miss Tarell."

" My dear Miss Courtenay, pray excuse her," said Lady Augusta.

" O, I've no doubt Miss Courtenay will for-give her," said Lady Dartmore, rising; " but I fancy we shall none of us be ready for din-ner—this is Liberty Hall, I think."

Constance was gone before the conclusion of this speech, Miss Tarell saying to her, as they crossed the hall, " But are you really going to be married to Sir Charles? You're very cross to him, I think."

" Miss Courtenay is very right to go to her toilet first," said Lady Dartmore, " for she's a person who would be nothing without dress."

" She dresses beautifully," said Miss Tribe.

" I don't agree with your ladyship, in thinking that she would look ill in any dress, or under any circumstances," said Sir Charles ; " she is one of the most beautiful girls that I ever saw : her beauty is of the most lasting character, for it is repléte with intelligence. But I hold her to be proud to a degree, and heartless."

" You do ?—I'm charmed to find that your eyes are opened at last ; but depend upon it she is not aware of the opinion you have of her, but thinks you admire her greatly."

" Perhaps she's right," said Sir Charles, with a sigh ; and he went away, muttering to himself, " To doubt, yet doat, suspect, yet fondly love."

Constance entered her own apartment in a state of excited feeling, which she vainly struggled to repress. She was not one of those young ladies who would sit down and indulge in a good fit of crying, but she endeavoured to cool down her wrath, and to mitigate her vexation, by walking up and down the room, until the last moment when Mitten came to dress her.

" You're looking quite poorly to-day, miss," was the maid's consolatory ejaculation.

" Am I?" said Constance, scarcely listening to what she said.

" But then," resumed Mitten, " that Lady Dartmore makes every other body look sickly. It's like putting a full crimson silk to match agen a pale pink. No offence, miss; but then she wears a pound of rouge on them cheeks of her's, as her woman often tells me."

" You should not encourage Lady Dartmore's maid in speaking scandal of her mistress," said Constance, rather sharply.

" Lord-a-mercy, ma'am ! there's no harm in talking of what a lady wears, I suppose; why, you would call this here scandal, I suppose ;— no offence; but as I was following her lady-ship up stairs last night—you know, miss, she's admired for her wondrous white neck— her gownd had slipped a little off them shoulders of her's—it's low enough at all times — Well, to be sure, if her back wasn't covered with pearl powder, and just where her gownd had slipped was a rim of her own natural skin, good enough, if her ladyship wouldn't deface God's works with them paints."

" Why, Mitten, you are quite corrupted

since you have known Lady Dartmore's woman. But dress me quickly, there's a good creature, for I hear the last bell."

" Why, you knows, miss, I am not used to them there artifices. My misses, bless her old bones, never knew the value of a pin's point of paint, and before I had the handling of you I never had nothing under sixty to dress. There, you're done up now, miss, and I'll warrant you'll look as well as any on 'em."

Constance endeavoured, and successfully, to get as far away as possible from Sir Charles and the grandees, at dinner. She saw little of them, for she was buried between two fat Miss Tribes, who made a sort of barricado for her. She was therefore enabled to be as silent as she pleased, for each of her neighbours was occupied with a beau on either side.

" Hetty," screamed the worthy Mrs. Tribe, " I hope you're taking care of Miss Courtenay."

" Miss Courtenay has eaten nothing, mama."

" Nor spoken ten words either," said Mr. Puzzleby, who sat opposite, in a quizzing tone, intended to raise her spirits by the honour of his notice.

" When pensive I thought of my love,"· whispered Lady Dartmore to Sir Charles ; but the witticism drew forth no smile.

The evening passed away much in the same manner as the day: nevertheless, Sir Charles prolonged his stay till a late hour, although he scarcely ever addressed himself to Constance. And in his semblance of indifference he completely excelled her, for he had been far more practised in society than she had, his nature was less ingenuous than hers, and his heart less warm to those whom he loved. Before the close of this painful day, Constance found herself unable to sustain the composure and indifference which she had assumed in the morning; she was mortified, disappointed, and indignant, and her countenance, towards the last, expressed so much dejection, that every one observed it.

" Come, you're all so very sombre to-night," said Lady Dartmore, " that to rouse you I will indulge you with one of my new Italian songs." She opened the piano, greatly to the surprise and scandal of the elder portion of the party, who would as soon have thought of turning

Jews, as of listening to profane music on a Sunday.

" And now my song is over," said Lady Dartmore, after executing a difficult bravura in the same obstreperous, over-done style as that in which all her actions were performed, " who will follow my example? Miss Courtenay, I know you sing," (wishing to challenge a comparison with herself.)

" Not to-night," said Constance, with as little of the tone of superior righteousness as she could help.

" Why not? Come, just to show that you owe no malice to Sir Charles and me for what happened this morning. You know he's very fond of music."

" Excuse me, Lady Dartmore, I cannot to-night."

" What! could you not give us something that would please Captain Powis?—' When first I saw your face,' or ' The Soldier's Dream?' "

" I would rather not, my lady."

" Nay, you must not get into the habit of refusing people. I have heard that your voice is charming; is it not, Sir Charles?"

" I have never sung when Sir Charles has been present," answered Constance, for she was resolved not to accept of any compliment from him.

" No," said Sir Charles, " I am aware that you have never done me the honour to sing to me, Miss Courtenay; it was from Bouverie that I knew how much you excelled in that accomplishment."

" Come now, you've no excuse," resumed Lady Dartmore, taking Miss Courtenay's hand. Constance almost shrunk back.

" If you will force me to give my reasons," said she, " do not suppose that I mean to make reflections on any one else; but I never do sing upon a Sunday, except it be sacred music."

" Pretty little well-tutored school-girl," exclaimed Lady Dartmore, scornfully. " That's all cant," whispered she to Sir Charles.

" Pardon me, I do not think so; I believe Miss Courtenay to be incapable of saying any thing which she does not think," said Sir Charles, aloud.

Constance felt the generosity of this defence.

" Since you are fond of music, Sir Charles,

perhaps you will not think one of our old an-
thems too solemn," said she, taking off her gloves.

" By no means; I delight in them, and am
only too happy that you should think me
worthy to listen to one of them."

" Why, that I don't know," returned Constance, with much simplicity, shaking her head.

" It is better to be abused by you, Miss
Courtenay," said Sir Charles, bending down
to place the music-book, " than to be met
with that freezing coldness with which I have
been treated by you all day. I trust you don't
mean to give me a second edition of it."

" Why, that cannot be called a second edition which is only a continuation of the first
part of the work," replied Constance, trying not
to melt towards him, nor to meet the expressive
glances of his eyes.

" Tell me what I shall sing."

" Let us have ' Hear my prayer,' for that is
emblematical," said Sir Charles.

" Alas!" replied Constance, " that speech
shows how little your mind is attuned to the
sentiment of this song. I, too, shall not be
able to do it justice."

She got through it, however, with tolerable composure until she came to that part, "O that I had wings like a dove; then would I flee away, and be at rest!" The thought that she had been deceived by the person dearest to her —even a wish that the close of a life, for which no one seemed to care, might not be distant:— both these ideas passed in quick succession through her mind. She stopped, and turning to Sir Charles, saw that his eyes were full of tears.

"Why—what's this?" said Lady Dartmore, coming forward; "here's a dead stand."

"I must return home," said Sir Charles, hastily; "the night is far advanced. Miss Courtenay, can I have the honour of executing any commands for you in London? You have a younger sister there, I think."

"Yes; but she is at school, and I have no other friend there, or any where else," said Constance, scarcely able to restrain a burst of tears, for resentfully as she had felt towards Sir Charles, she felt as if his departure would render existence almost a blank to her.

"May I hope that our unaccountable differences," said the young Baronet, in a low tone, his voice trembling with emotion, " may be suspended till we meet again, when all may, perhaps, be explained?"

" Captain Powis, make haste here," said Lady Dartmore, "if you do not wish your fair friend to be run off with. I absolutely think Sir Charles will carry her away to London."

Constance gave a look of indignation, Captain Powis was sulky, and a dead silence for a few instants prevailed in the party.

" Your horses are at the door, Sir Charles," broke the spell, and then adieux, and good wishes, and much bustle, ushered the Baronet to the hall door.

Constance was this time happy, when she found herself once more in her antiquated bed-chamber; the seclusion of Newberry seemed, as it were, Paradise to her, compared to the indignities which she had suffered at Mr. Tribe's. She determined henceforward to drive Sir Charles from her thoughts, to devote her time to improvement, to charity, to her religious duties. She resolved to seek the advice of Mr. Bouverie

relative to the course which it was best for her
to pursue in the employment of her time.   She
felt more than ever that it was necessary to rest
upon herself for happiness.

CHAPTER XIII.

" On the tip of his subduing tongue,
All kind of arguments and questions deep,
All replication prompt, and reasons strong,
For his advantage still did wake and sleep."

SHAKSPEARE.

IT was on a fine, clear Sunday, about three weeks after Constance had returned from Mr. Tribe's, that Miss Monckton proposed to her to go to afternoon service at Ditton, a village about four miles from Newberry, to hear a sermon from the reverend and celebrated Dr. Clayton.

" You will see," said Miss Monckton, " a great curiosity. You will hear a great divine, you will be overpowered with a most prodigal use of fine words, and splendid comparisons, but you will come away more puzzled than edified. At the same time, I will promise to show you one of the most pleasing specimens of a middle-aged woman, my particular friend, Mrs. Clayton ; and, if we happen to be invited to stay dinner, which is the custom at Ditton parsonage, after service, you will meet with a whole bevy of remarkable persons."

"And why is this reverend gentleman so celebrated ?" inquired Constance.

"For the great mass of useless literary lumber of which his brain is the store-room," said Miss Monckton ; "for his eloquence in society, (for to call his manner of discoursing conversation, would be like comparing the proverbs of Solomon to a bon-mot,)—for his indiscreet and often pernicious interference in political affairs—for his unrivalled effrontery in choosing often to copy the furry inhabitants of the arctic region, in preference to adopting the manners of the human race. Yet, with all this, the old doctor is beloved."

"Nay, that surprizes me still more."

"There is in him that which, in the long run, ensures affection, although it often provokes satire—an unreserved manifestation of his character to the inspection of others : you see him as he really is. His vanity is egregious, yet he never attempts to veil it by any show of modesty. His animosities are violent; but he never indulges in their virulence under the mask of pretended friendship. His habits are gross; his conversation often indelicate; but he does not, like your modern gentlemen, couch his impurities under the flowery guise of sentimental virtue. But come and see him, and judge how you like him."

"After all," said Constance, as they stepped into their post-chaise, "I do not think you have given him a single good quality in your description."

"Have I not?—then I ought; for, though he is essentially disagreeable, he is universally benevolent. I do not mean that sort of universal benevolence, which extends itself to the West Indies, but does not expand at home; for that I conceive to be nothing more than a burlesque of charity:—I do love in the old doctor that neighbourly, old-fashioned feeling, which cannot see distress without offering present help. He will scold the poor man who imprudently marries, and brings a large family to squall and starve in the parish ; but that poor man will seldom want for soup from the doctor's table, or coals from his cellar. So eccentric, yet so unostentatious, is his benevolence, that his 'right hand knoweth not what his left doeth.' And he is an excellent parish clergyman. He has the most uncouth, yet the best mode of managing his tithe people that I ever saw ; and whilst other ministers are plunged into litigation, he is beloved in both his small livings."

" And is he hospitable also ?" said Constance.

" There now, you are thinking of your dinner ! Well, I can say, I think, he has the spirit of hospitality within him ; but it manifests itself outwardly in a strange manner. For instance, he likes to see his table crammed with guests, and, though he idolizes the rich and great, he is always sure to stuff in, at his ample, but inelegant board, those to whom he thinks a dinner may be acceptable. The curate, upon a fifty pound stipend—the schoolmaster without scholars—the briefless barrister—sometimes even the strolling player—and not unfrequently the pragmatical dissenting minister—

are there to be seen in contiguity with the peer or the bishop, the judge, or the great John Kemble. But we are coming to the village. That is the church—a pretty, ancient, well-preserved edifice, as you see. Listen to the bells—are they not melodious? Now, you little think that you are hearing in them the voices of the apostles themselves. In imitation of monastic times, the doctor has baptized them. The great, deep, swinging tone belongs to St. Peter; the lesser one to St. Matthew; the next in power to St. Luke; the softer and sweet treble sound appertains to St. John. What are you about?"

"Oh! I do wish to walk along that pretty path to the church," said Constance. "I love a corn-field approach to a church; so pray stop the driver, that I may get out."

"By no means; the doctor likes to see carriages drive up to the door. It reminds him of former times, when the great men of his generation paid him the compliment to crowd his afternoon service. But now I consider him as somewhat on the decline. He has been overrated, and sooner or later that is an evil which rectifies itself. But we are early: let us take a look into the church before the congregation assembles."

It was now that hour of the winter's day, when nature, and the objects of art by which she is defaced or embellished, are revealed to us in a softened light. Already the cottage fires blazed with a brightened flame in the village, as the careful housewife replenished the grate preparatory to her early tea. When the two ladies entered Ditton church, a partial gloom obscured its narrow aisles, although the rich streams of the setting sun glanced athwart the chancel, emblazoning, but with a transitory radiance, the painted window, rescued during the French Revolution from the reliques of a chapel belonging to the Orleans family. Of this splendid, but somewhat patched and mu-tilated specimen of ancient art, the doctor was notoriously proud, although a rigid Protestant might deem its portraitures, if strictly inves-tigated, to have been misplaced in a church erected since the Reformation ; for the bishops, and dukes, and princes, and pious princesses, who had graced the illustrious line whom the paint-ing was destined to honour, were intermingled

with St. Laurences, St. Martins, St. Catherines,
St. Genevieves, St. Rosalies, and Holy Virgins,
with a profusion which, to say the truth, somewhat obscured the individuality of these sacred
personages. On each side of the altar were
figures of St. Mark and St. Luke, standing, it
may be presumed, in guardianship of its purity.
A small side window, with a beautiful paint-
ing on it of the pensive and benevolent countenance of Cranmer, might seem also intended to
reassert the supremacy of the reformed church,
had it not been placed opposite to the portrait
of Thomas Aquinas, in whom, when his cumbrous learning, his knotty metaphysics, and
jargonous language are considered, the doctor
might find a congenial spirit. On the whole,
the church resembled a papistical chapel far
more than the resort of the simple Protestant
congregation of Ditton. Independent of his
own taste, which led to decoration and clerical
display, the doctor was of opinion that too
many of the catch-traps to devotion, so sedulously preserved in the Romish church, have
been abandoned in our present worship; and
held it good to sacrifice something to the weak-

nesses of human nature, on a point whereon, alas! it is of all others prone to be weak.

Two marble tablets, on either side of the altar, were consecrated to the memory of the doctor's only children—two daughters, who had died, one in early youth, the other in the maturity of a weary existence, after she had become a wife and mother. Their epitaphs, though written with much pedantry, and with some parental exaggeration of their attractions and virtues, were affecting; for what monumental tribute from a bereaved father to his children would not be affecting? And besides, these blossoms of his existence, early culled by inscrutable decree, had displayed much that could engage a parent's love, and justify his pride; and when I say that they were extolled in too pompous terms, I mean to imply that few human beings could merit the high-sounding epithets which the doctor bestowed upon the *victims* of his praise—for as victims, the objects of injudicious praise may be considered.

The bells ceased; and Miss Monckton and Constance were shown into a high-backed, well-lined pew—the doctor's own dormitory, when others preached or prayed. In a short time, the beadle poured in upon them, from an adjacent repository, bibles and prayer-books almost as large as themselves. Anon entered the good doctor himself; and Constance, as the service had not begun, had time to contemplate this extraordinary personage.

He was a bulky man, of about sixty years of age, but in the full vigour of a constitution which neither his habits of profound thought, nor of immoderate eating, had as yet, in any great degree, impaired. Perhaps this might be in some measure owing to his constant early rising, and to his residence in pure air, and among people of simple manners. Nothing of age was as yet visible in the dark grey lustre of his eye, which, whether it brightened with benevolence, or flashed with anger, or softened with the influence of reflection, or melted with the recollections of former days, conveyed to all, the impression that he, whose most expressive feature thus varied, was, indeed, no common man. His eyes were shaded by eyebrows of great magnitude, and a nose, vast in proportion, rose above cheeks, swelled out by self-indulgence, and the contentment of a disposition naturally blithe and jovial. The mouth was remarkably compressed, and the upper lip somewhat receding; the expression of the dogmatist, the unflinching disputant, the demolisher of all inferior wits—in short, of the petted lion of society, being strongly conveyed by the marked feature of this organ. A complexion usually of a greyish tinge, was this afternoon heightened by the exertion of bustling up the aisle in full canonicals, of which none displayed a more ample, and spurious collection on his own person, than the reverend Dr. Clayton. Denied the mitre by adverse fate, he yet chose to assume the cassock, and, with his standing-out, well-powdered wig, containing hair enough to stuff a moderate sized pillow, he looked in the eyes of his simple parishioners, of far more importance than any bishop they had ever seen. Constance, however, observed, that the wags of country bumpkins, winked, and laughed together slily, as the Doctor, with much pomposity, passed them, and mounted the reading-desk; nor could she, without difficulty, keep her own gravity, when a

message came to Miss Monckton during the abso-
lution, importing that " there was a good round
of boiled beef at the rectory, and he hoped that
she and her young friend would stay and dine
there." A general irreverent titter shook the
whole congregation, when the doctor, after the
first lesson, exhorted them all, with much so-
lemnity, as they valued his safety, not to kill
their pigs after the usual mode on the high-
way, as his horse had been startled by the
squeaking of one of these Christmas victims, and
recommended the dismissal of these animals
from the world by the Yorkshire method, namely,
" knocking them on the head." Yet the inhabitants of Ditton were accustomed to exhorta-
tions equally misplaced, for few clergymen have
been known to take such liberties with divine
service, as the learned Dr. Clayton.

His reading was most remarkable ; saving
a lisp, which he could control at pleasure,
his voice was fine, and his ear acute to the
niceties of modulation. Some passages, however, of the service he galloped over with a ra-
pidity which defied attention ; others he gave,
with a startling emphasis, which was either fine,

or ludicrous, according to the state of mind of the hearer, but which was generally offensive to him who "went to pray," and wished not to "remain to scoff." It was his custom also to interlard the lessons with such phrases as these : " That's wrong." " The original runs thus." " My brethren, this text was introduced by such and such prelates, for such and such controversial purposes." Thus unsettling the minds of his usually humble readers, without, in all probability, succeeding in setting them right again.

After a learned yet desultory, heavy yet at times, eloquent, unintelligible sermon in the Doctor's best lisp, Miss Monckton and Constance, ushered forth by Sam, major-domo of the church and rectory, proceeded to pay their respects to Mrs. Clayton, who had been desired by the Doctor to "stay at home and mind the dinner." They were, however, overtaken by the divine, and Constance duly introduced to his portly holiness.

" Miss Courtenay, did you say ? Miss Courtenay—one of the Courtenays of Devon ?" asked the doctor, who loved any one with a

tolerable pedigree, ten times as well as one without produceable ancestry.

" No, sir, I believe of Norfolk."

" A very good family that," said the Doctor,
" though neither so ancient nor so high in blood
as the other. You will soon part with your name,
I will venture to prophesy; but mind you tell
your father, or brother, or cousin, or whoever is
the ostensible head of your respectable line—
tell them, I say, not to disgrace so ancient, so
gentle, and so honourable a name!"

Constance was almost frightened.

" I grieve, sir, to say, I must apply your
advice to myself, for I am almost the last who
bears my name."

" Then, madam, since the branches of the
tree are lopped off, I advise you to graft yourself upon a new stock forthwith.— But where is
that rascal Jack?" said he, looking back im-
periously towards a fat, slovenly-looking man,
who walked submissively behind him. "Jack!"
said the doctor, in a voice which might have
charged a regiment, " make up to Miss Courtenay—make yourself agreeable to her, man.
Don't wait till you're fifty before you put the

final question.. For, Miss Courtenay," said he, in solemn tone, " Jack is a most benevolent man—Jack is a most learned man—Jack *was* a very handsome man—Jack *has* been a most loveable man—but Jack is a shy man, and cannot tell a lady his mind. Jack, I command you to marry."

Jack, as he was called, had too long been a boon companion, a satellite, though not a parasite of the doctor, to remonstrate against the unwarrantable liberty taken with one of his age and profession, for he was a clergyman. The comforts of a profitable benefice, and the indulgence of a disposition naturally indolent, and habitually, from his initiation into a college fellowship, luxurious, had obscured the real powers and attainments of the reverend John, or, as he was commonly called, Jack Bamford. Still there were gleams of native intelligence, and indications of former study, even in a countenance every line of which was embedded in right good ecclesiastical fat. He was almost the only gratuitous and disinterested friend that the Doctor possessed ; for, by the great, Doctor Clayton was courted as a necessary appendage to their literary acquaintance; by the learned, much for the same reason that a cook prizes a receipt book, to refer to; by persons of his own rank, too often for what they could get out of him either in the way of patronage, or influence, or by the more direct mode of his own ready munificence. But honest John, or Jack, really loved him: was blind to his outrageous defects, in love with his virtues, revered his learning, and in short, " honoured the shadow of his shoe-tie."

" There now," said Miss Monckton, as Constance and she waited a few minutes in the hall to take off their bonnets, " you are destined for a clergyman's wife. All Newberry gives you to Mr. Bouverie, and Dr. Clayton fixes on Mr. Bamford for you."

" Mr. Bouverie I will never have, and Mr. Bamford is much more suited to you than to me," said Constance.

" So I think; but she who marries Mr. Bamford must marry Dr. Clayton also. Must have him ordering his own dinner, and fixing his own party, smoking his pipe in your drawing-room, and scolding his friend's wife, a privilege with which, I think, husbands should never part."

"And what made your friend Mrs. Clayton marry the very head and front of all this offending?" asked Constance.

"Hush—why," (in a whisper,) "I cannot exactly tell you.   Too probably, for a home : for Mary Stapleton, at the age of forty-five, was probably sick, like many other single maidens, of visiting her friends—of having to condole with one, to nurse the other, to keep a third in good humour.   To see children spoiled without the luxury of whipping them, to find servants impertinent without the power of discharging them.   It is, in short, living by deputy.   But come, you will see now what she has got in exchange for her former lot."   So saying they entered the sitting-room.

CHAPTER XIV.

Heaven rest his saul, whare'er he be !
Is the wish o' mony mae than me:
He had twa fauts, or may be three,
                    Yet what remead ?
A social, honest man want we.

Burns.

Ditton Rectory was a large, staring, red brick house, without the smallest attempt at elegance or decoration without. A small palisaded garden in front separated it from the road. To the right, conspicuous enough, was the doctor's summer-house, where he studied, and wrote, and dogmatized to Jack, and oftener smoked through the long day, when not interrupted by visitors. It was when emerging from this retreat to receive two bishops, who paid him the homage of a visit, that a mischievous pupil of his, an inmate, had stuck into the protuberance of his unconscious wig two turkey feathers, which, as he bowed and bowed, with many set and courtly phrases, overpowered the decorum and gravity of the right reverend prelates, one of whom, being a wag, afterwards compared the learned doctor to a turkey coming forth from a hen-roost. Having surmounted the recollection of this joke, the doctor to his dying day was wont to pour forth volumes of smoke, and to indite volumes of equally *subtle* fabrication in this beloved sanctum, where, indeed, alone he was emperor.

The doctor had been twice married, as our reader may have already inferred, and he had only very recently, by a second nuptial, relinquished the glory of being talked of for many ladies, both high and low. His first wife was a termagant, little less clever than himself— equally eloquent, and quite as fond of talking. As they never happened to agree, except in hating each other, disputes from the top and bottom of the dinner-table often ran high; but the doctor was usually compelled to give in. Of course, he resolved to revenge himself for this domestic usurpation on his second consort; and having been long usher of the black rod at one of the most celebrated of our public schools, he had sufficient of the leaven of tyranny in his composition within him to brow-beat any woman —except his first wife.

Notwithstanding his early grievances, he never failed, publicly and privately, and especially in the presence of the second Mrs. Clayton, to extol the memory of her predecessor; and Constance found him expatiating in a high tone upon her many virtues, and describing her as the "first of women" to a visitor, to whom he was showing her picture, wherein there seemed to common eyes to be developed as much of the shrew, in as upright a position, and as fierce a dress, as could be. The veritable Mrs. Clayton sat in a retired part of the room, with the utmost meekness depicted on a face still lovely, for scarcely a wrinkle, in these early days of her marriage, defaced the clearness of her fine skin, and her light hair was yet unchanged by time. She was a gentlewoman in every sense of the word, at least in the sense of people of that day, for the notions of a gentlewoman are changed since then. Forgetful of self, deferential to the old, benevolent and even playful with the young, dignified yet not repulsive to the other sex, kind to her servants, dutiful to her husband, devout to her God;— few persons could view Mrs. Clayton, even in these early days of her marriage, without lamenting that her " lines had not fallen in pleasant places." She soon found out that her influence with the Doctor was at zero—her controul over his servants just a shadow of authority—her hopes of domestic comfort a dream. Having been shackled all her life by kind, interfering friends and well-meaning relations, who generally plague single women out of their lives, she now, when she had hoped for emancipation, found herself a very slave indeed. Nevertheless, she resolved not to murmur, made the best of every thing, endeavoured to persuade herself that it was only the doctor's way, and was eventually rewarded by the felicity—of surviving him.

Constance directly took a fancy to this engaging woman, and the favourable impression was mutual; for Mrs. Clayton had seen a great deal of good society, and had thence acquired that intuitive discrimination which those who can profit by experience, obtain. She looked at Miss Courtenay with lively admiration, regretted in her own mind that so fair a flower should blossom that day at Ditton, where the dinner party accidentally assembled afforded, as she, in secret, thought, but little interest, unless the spirit of Grotius, or that of Duns Scotus, had been allowed to descend, and enjoy society congenial only to such souls as theirs.

Dinner was very soon announced, for the Doctor seemed to writhe with impatience until that blessed moment. He then led Miss Monckton into an ample, square apartment, which served the double purposes of library and dining-room. It was literally crammed with books, each of which owned a binding of moth-eaten aspect. Incalculable produce of human learning reposed upon these shelves, but little did the public, little did the *literati*, little did the Doctor's friends, suspect, that upon the marginal pages of his favourite classics he had inscribed the names and designated the characters of those who often unconsciously sat at his table, whilst they were handed down to posterity, sometimes in very dark colours, above.

The party assembled consisted, including the two stranger ladies, of ten persons. To the right of the doctor sat a thin, tall, sarcastic looking man, who appeared as if encased in an armour of his own self-esteem, which kept him from the contact of inferior beings. To him the Doctor chiefly addressed his conversation, and Constance soon made out that he was head master of a celebrated school—a man of eminent learning, and of the highest character in other respects. What was her surprise to find that the discourse of the two sapient Doctors, to whom she at first chiefly directed her attention, turned upon eating! Opposite to this gentleman sat the doctor's stipendiary toad-eater, the reverend but not revered Mr. Collins, and to this man Miss Courtenay took an instant and decided aversion. She afterwards learned that he had but recently been relieved from an ecclesiastical suspension, for some gross clerical misdemeanour. He looked, indeed, as if he had sneaked into society, and was fearful of being kicked out again. For this reason he dealt all sorts of compliments and civility around him with unremitting perseverance, notwithstanding the total indifference which he met with from all, and the contempt of some. To the Doctor he furnished a constant butt, on which to shoot the arrows of his wit, or the stings of his ill-humour. To call him " fool," " ass," "dunce," seemed to the Doctor as natural as to speak to him by his proper name, yet it was remarkable that even in his most unguarded and irritated moments he never, in the most distant terms, alluded to the calamity from which Mr. Collins had been recently emancipated, or to the poverty which had partly been the result of that mishap. This might be faint praise in others; but in Doctor Clayton it was an instance of uncommon forbearance. Opposite to her father sat Miss Collins, his daughter—a dark-haired, fair, and rather plump, and pretty young person, of about two-and-twenty. The black and sparkling eyes of this damsel expressed considerable shrewdness, but betrayed a jealous, and restless tenacity of the jokes and civil insults constantly played off upon her father, towards whom, whilst she never spoke to him without a sort of corrective sharpness, she evinced an affection, which was the only gentle part of her character. This young lady had had, what was then an uncommon advantage, a classical education, having been educated with her brothers; and had acquired sufficient Latin and Greek to make her formidable to her own sex, and an object of ridicule to Dr. Clayton; for in those days, and perhaps in these, the greater the learning of the tyrant of the domestic board, the stronger his aversion to his woman-kind knowing more than how to sew a seam, or manufacture a pudding.

The acquirements of Miss Collins were, therefore, a source of constant raillery to the Doctor, who considered himself privileged to banter the whole family in virtue of their father's submission to his sway ; but he found in the spirited girl a stout resistance to his indignities. Hence he partly disliked, partly feared her, and it was only when he was very much out of humour, that he plagued her by bringing forward to public notice the learning of which Miss Collins was so much ashamed. Beside Agnes Collins, sat a gentleman considerably younger than the rest of the company, which circumstance authorized him, as he thought, to flirt with Miss Collins, and to stare at Miss Courtenay. The dark and wicked eyes of this person, his arched, marked eyebrows, quizzical turned-up nose, and satirical mouth, gave Constance the impression that he was a lawyer. But, alas! he was a clergyman also. And he was a living instance of one of those crying sins, which, of all others, contributed perhaps most to the indifference to religion which peculiarly prevailed towards the close of the eigthteenth century. He was forced, against his inclination and his conscience, to take orders from what, to his father, was an all-convincing reason, the certainty of obtaining a good living,—a calculation made without taking eternity into account. The result of such unprincipled conduct is too frequent to require much comment. Young Wakley professed, and felt, reluctance to be " dubbed a saint," and went through the requisite ordeal with some pangs of conscience ; but, having accomplished all necessary forms, he declared his resolution to play a part no longer. Accordingly he gave himself licence to what Shakspeare has mis-named the " pleasant vices," and practised every sin but that of hypocrisy. To his Curate and his Sexton he devolved all weekly concerns, contented with mouthing out, on each revolving Sunday, a piece of oratory justly his own, because he had paid for it; but which had no other effect on the minds of his hearers than to call their attention to the wild career of the individual who addressed them, and to act as a flourish of trumpets before his deeds of the next week. With all this, Mr. Wakley was, unfortunately, of a character not to be disliked by the vulgar judges of his merits. He was good-natured, profuse in his hospitality and donations, and remarkably easy to the sins of others; and he had an off-hand way of alluding to, and half confessing his faults, which many people mistook for candour—whilst it was only impudence.

Such was the man, who by some general acquirements, by a degree of ready wit, by much obsequiousness, and by persevering good humour, had recommended himself to the favour of the learned Dr. Clayton. As Constance had never seen any of these persons before, she had the pleasing occupation of finding out their characters; and, although not very experienced

in such studies, she soon became disgusted with
Mr. Collins and Mr. Wakley, though for different reasons, and in different degrees. She
considered herself fortunate in being seated
beside Mr. Bamford, who, though by no means
insensible to the charms of an animated and artless girl, thought Miss Courtenay too much his
junior to treat her with any of those tender
advances which the Doctor had recommended,
but behaved to her much the same as if she had
just come from the nursery; helped her to the
nicest things, answered her in a caressing, encouraging sort of tone, and saw that she was
properly attended to by the servants. In truth,
this was no easy matter at Ditton Rectory,
where a species of actual republican govern-
ment prevailed, for Doctor Clayton was only
the nominal monarch. The chief members of
the legislature were the man-servant and the
cook; the man had for many years held the
multifarious offices of groom, valet, master of
the robes, inspector of the wigs, coachman,
gardener, butler, brewer, footman, and keeper
to the old Doctor, who could neither ride,
smoke, dress, preach, visit, receive visitors, nor

travel, without "Sam" at his elbow. Although
we must acknowledge that Sam's merits were
great, we may, without detraction to that in-
fluential personage, remark that, like many
other ministerial characters, ancient and modern, he had come to the pass of thinking that
the world could scarcely go round without him.
Whether mounted on the coach-box, or attend-
ant to his master on horseback, or bustling in
with the dinner-things, or frizzing the doctor's
wigs, or combating his whims, there was on
Sam's features that look of unalterable self-complacency which is, perhaps, the supreme point
of felicity. By force of habit, and of a little
common sense, he had, indeed, acquired a degree
of control over his gifted master, without which,
or upon the slightest abatement, Sam was ready,
like ministers, to relinquish his post instantly.

The other member of the administration
/was   visible only in the watery soup, hard
potatoes, half-boiled fish, and over-roasted
mutton which she sent to table, and on which
points neither Mrs. Clayton nor the doctor
dared to offer a word. For, as it is said, was
the case with a recently deceased gastronome,

the Doctor's table, despite his genuine love of its real pleasures, was execrably managed. A profusion, indeed, prevailed, but it was a profusion which his guests would gladly have exchanged for one well-dressed, wholesome dish : and the only sense which the doctor showed of what was really good in an epicurean sense, was in choosing what was acknowledged by all to be, and what was actually the best dish, for his own peculiar eating. But the age of refined criticism in such matters, had not yet arrived.

Poor Mrs. Clayton sat at the head of her table, with a painful perception of the errors of the whole concern painted on her face, and sometimes, but hopelessly, endeavoured to arrest the torrent of blunders.

" Sam, you had better leave the fish a little longer," said she, in accents as gentle as those of a seraph. Sam carried it away.

" Sam, bring me that sweet-bread."

" The Doctor has the sweet-bread, ma'am, it can't be moved."

" Sam, ask for some more potatoes." No answer.

" Sam, we want some more port wine."

" There's enough port decantered ma'am."

" Sam, do not take the cloth off just yet." Sam cleared it off without deigning to give a reason.

If the Doctor liked any one lady at table, in particular, it was Miss Monckton; in the first place, she was well born, and then she had a ready, authoritative way of answering him which kept him in trim, and which he really liked in women; and it is questionable whether he ever had any real regard for the regiment of sycophants who relieved guard at his table. As a mark of his peculiar favour, he always addressed her by her christian name.

" Jane Monckton," he said, " does thy weak head remember that I met that clever girl, Maria Edgeworth, lately?"

" Remember it! Why you only told me last week, Doctor."

" And did I tell thee, thou saucy jade, the speech which the pert lass made to me, and the answer which I gave her? Ay! it was well done."

" Then let us hear what it was, Doctor."

" The prattling puss!—he, he, he, he!"
The doctor's laugh was indescribable *then*:
now we might compare it to the steam escaping from a boiler:—it was between a hiss
and a cry. " 'Doctor,' said she, as we sat down
to table, ' I know you dislike me vastly.' Now
I thought she wanted discretion in challenging
me, Dr. Clayton, to single combat, and doubtless she displayed a great want of Christian
charity in attacking me before dinner, and
before such a dinner ; and, therefore, I replied
to her thus :—' Madam ! I never contradict a
lady ?' "

A burst of laughter from Mr. Collins followed the relation of this piece of incivility ;
but Miss Monckton coolly answered,

" Indeed I think it was a great pity that she
did challenge you, Doctor, since you didn't
know how to behave yourself."

" Jane Monckton, thou shalt rue this,"
thought the Doctor ; but not caring to vent his
spleen upon one who answered him so fearlessly,
he indulged his ill-humour upon poor Miss
Collins. The gentleman whom we first des-

cribed, having quoted Juvenal, thought proper to apologize, to the ladies for it. " I confess myself guilty," said he, pragmatically, " of a literary misdemeanour : I submit to the decision of the fair : any thing but banishment from their presence, even if I be doomed to lock up Horace for the space of six months, or if sentence of transportation be passed upon Ovid for a year !"

" How now," said the Doctor. " How are we to get out of this dilemma ?" looking towards Miss Collins, who immediately drew back, and half concealed herself between the two gentlemen, her neighbours. " Come forth, Agnes Collins;" said he, " the sentence is nullified if there be one lady in company who can translate Juvenal ; and you, a well-instructed, diligent, docile pupil of your *gifted* father—you, the Miss Carter of our intellectual county—you, a most accomplished, most learned lady, you can rescue my enlightened friend, this elegant scholar, and pious divine, from the heavy trammels under which he incautiously has placed himself." A pause ensued. " Agnes Collins, translate !" said the Doctor, who was waxing warm, that his capricious commands were not obeyed.

All those who possessed any feeling, were distressed for the poor girl who was thus rendered conspicuous upon a score respecting which her feelings were needlessly tender. In this emergency Mr. Wakley gallantly stepped forth to take the ridicule of the company upon himself. He made a hasty translation, in which there was some error, trivial, and perhaps scarcely obvious to common people, but of vast magnitude with critics. The doctor burst into a passion of laughter which can only be faintly described by comparing it to the whirring of a bottle of soda water, when the cork is violently extracted. His laughter, for many reasons, was generally contagious; and when a calm succeeded, it was employed in verbal criticisms and discussions, provoked by Mr. Wakley's error, and these lasted until the ladies withdrew.

The Doctor's friends always went away early from the rectory, and Constance, and her friend, found themselves on the road to New-berry soon after eight o'clock. It was a fine starry night, and they amused themselves, during a great part of the way, as most people do, in talking over the peculiarities of the company whom they had left. At length, Miss Monckton suddenly changed the conversation, and said, in her abrupt way; "I wonder what has become of Sir Charles Marchmont; I think he has deserted Newberry."

"Perhaps," said Constance, trusting to the darkness of the night to conceal her countenance, "he is gone to see Miss Herbert."

"Oh, you believe that story," said Miss Monckton; "for my part, I do not. I am sure Sir Charles's heart is free, or was free, a few months ago. I have no faith in early engagements, or early attachments in these days. But who told you this fine history?"

"It was Lady Dartmore."

"Then it is sure not to be true—she has no notion of truth at all—she is a walking falsehood. I don't believe a word of it," said Miss Monckton, three or four times over, and not without irritation, for she secretly wished, and earnestly believed that Sir Charles was in love with Miss Courtenay.

CHAPTER XV.

Beamless is the eye, and closed in night, which looked serenity, and sweetness, and love. The face that was to us
as the face of an angel, is mangled and deformed; the
heart that glowed with the purest fire, and beat with
the best affections, is now become a clod of the valley.

LOGAN'S SERMONS.

CONSTANCE had often regretted the change
which had been, during some weeks, apparent
in the conduct of Mr. Bouverie towards her.
Since the interference of the Newberry coteries,
he had seemed rather to shun, than to seek her.
It was true, that his manners to her were ever
respectful, polite, and even benevolent: and
there was no appearance of the pique and playful malice which had appeared in Sir Charles's
behaviour to her when under Mr. Tribe's roof.
Sometimes, indeed, it occurred to Constance,
that Mr. Bouverie felt an interest in her, which
was at variance with his studied avoidance of all

intimate converse : but this thought she pre-
sently discarded as a symptom of vanity, of
which the recent desertion of Sir Charles ought
to have cured her.   Touching that gentleman,
sundry reports prevailed. One was, that he was
really married, and was spending the honey-moon
at Bath.   Another, that he had gone abroad to
seek out his mother's place of interment, in
order that he might sell the old Priory, and
leave Newberry for ever.   All the good people
there were mortified at his absence ; and Mrs.
De Courcy in particular was disconsolate—but
finding it convenient to pay a long deferred visit
to London, at this time, she set off for the metropolis, a speculation of her's which served to
pass away the long evenings which Miss Pearson and the Miss Seagraves would otherwise
have found gloomy and insipid.   As none of
these ladies had ever been in London, they spoke
of it just as they would of Newberry.   " Well,
now, I wonder if Mrs. De Courcy has met Sir
Charles to-day. I have no doubt but that they
have been walking together.   I should suppose
they go to the same church—and I will make
bold to say, before now, he has seen her in that

new yellow dress, and admired her more than enough."

But alas ! after a month's visitation in a dull, cold, inhospitable house in Guildford Street, and after a full experience of the dirt, self-denial, and semi-darkness, to which London people, are, in many instances, subjected, Mrs. De Courcy returned to Newberry without once having seen Sir Charles, or heard any thing more of him than the name of the street in which he had been living. Still, he was an object of incessant discussion. It is impossible to deny that Constance did also sometimes think of him, for young ladies are apt to think on subjects which their better judgment bids them to forget. It is likewise true that she loved to saunter through the Priory Park, and that she sometimes looked up at the windows of his now deserted house with melancholy retrospection.

"But why should I even remember him at all?" said she to herself. "Our acquaintance has been as fleeting as a dream, and as fallacious also. By this time he has forgotten it, and surely it is worse than folly in me ever to give it a thought."

Spring was now fast disclosing the many varied hues of the mantle with which she invests all Nature. Constance had not, during the months of winter, forgotten the comforts of old Rose. Her cottage had been warmed by the lavish gifts of Miss Courtenay, her bed had been replenished by her bounty. The old woman acknowledged these inconsiderate presents with the more pleasure, that the hand which bestowed them had, in its mode of giving, nothing of the ostentatious Benevolent society-like manner which, whilst it extracts a gratitude which is with difficulty squeezed out, is often succeeded by a sort of moral nausea in the mind of the person obliged. Constance was amply repaid her exertions to benefit her aged charge, by the delightful consciousness smoothed the rugged path of age but in the interest which she long stories, and the instruction derived in gleaning from her rience of a life of vicissitude. afterwards look back on her brook, and the hours she had cottage, as those, if not the

the most unmixed with sorrow in her life.

One afternoon, however, their conversati
upon a theme of much melancholy inter
was the death of poor Susan. There
nothing remarkable in the story—it is
one of too frequent occurrence, but it w
effect of certain circumstances upon the
the humble heroine of the tale, that was,
dering her lowly sphere, somewhat unc
She was the lovely and only daughter of
Rose, and had been nurtured with infinit
although with much simplicity, in the
she had first seen the light. Sus..
and beauty of the family, and wh
r consented to her taking charge f
a lady of high birth, a cousin
March she felt that she ws
he good of her chil,
went—the
pe, hap
ealth, a
us mat
trust i
r's fr

Spring was now fast disclosing the many varied hues of the mantle with which she invests all Nature. Constance had not, during the months of winter, forgotten the comforts of old Rose. Her cottage had been warmed by the lavish gifts of Miss Courtenay, her bed had been replenished by her bounty. The old woman acknowledged these considerate presents with the more pleasure, that the hand which bestowed them had, in its mode of giving, nothing of the ostentatious Benevolent society-like manner which, whilst it extracts a gratitude which is with ffidiculty squeezed out, is often succeeded by a sort of moral nausea in the mind of the person obliged. Constance was amply repaid for her exertions to benefit her aged charge, not only by the delightful consciousness of having smoothed the rugged path of age and poverty, but in the interest which she took in Rose's long stories, and the instruction even which she derived in gleaning from her some of the experience of a life of vicissitude. Often did she afterwards look back on her walks to Birdbrook, and the hours she had passed in Rose's cottage, as those, if not the happiest, at least the most unmixed with sorrow in her early life.

One afternoon, however, their conversation ran upon a theme of much melancholy interest—it was the death of poor Susan. There was nothing remarkable in the story—it is perhaps one of too frequent occurrence, but it was the effect of certain circumstances upon the mind of the humble heroine of the tale, that was, considering her lowly sphere, somewhat uncommon. She was the lovely and only daughter of poor Rose, and had been nurtured with infinite care, although with much simplicity, in the village where she had first seen the light. Susan was the pride and beauty of the family, and when her mother consented to her taking charge of the infant of a lady of high birth, a cousin of Sir Charles Marchmont, she felt that she was sacrificing to the supposed good of her child, her own last comfort. She went—the young and innocent girl—elate with hope, happy in a guileless heart, blooming with health, and just with enough knowledge of religious matters to know that she must fear God, and trust in Him. A foreboding shook the poor mother's frame as she parted from the darling of her desolate old age, and saw her cross the threshold for the last time. But she went, and old Rose was left alone, to sit and think in her cottage of many summer and winter days of happiness with this her last stay, of fond and anxious gazings upon the cherub face of her Susan's infancy, of the felicity of returned affection in the more matured season of her child's life. Alas! what mother cannot perfect the picture of hope and love, love amounting to rapture, which her own feelings may supply? After a year or more of wistful thoughts of the absent, of eager watchings for the post-boy, of delight at the casual intelligence of travellers, the letters from Susan became first short and sad,—then rare,—then ceased altogether. The mother tried to bear delays, to hope, to be resigned to the neglect of her darling, if she were happy, reproached her not, and endeavoured to wile away the languor of an existence without that object to cheer it which it once had possessed.

At last a letter arrived. Susan was coming home; yet the announcement of her journey sounded strange in Rose's ear.

" Mother," she wrote, " take me home again; I will work for you, obey you, attend you more than ever, till I die."

She came, and her mother had her treasure back again: but was it Susan—was it the laughing, bounding girl, whose fleetness defied that of her young competitors in the dance and the race, whose dark blue eye, restless from the overflowings of a happy heart, only varied in its expression of felicity from the calmness of contentment to the sparkling gleams of joy? An emaciated, drooping creature, her frame at times shaken by a short, but hard and mer- ciless cough, her pallid lips scarcely forming themselves into a forced smile, her eyes cast down with shame or hopeless grief, or raised in agony to her mother's face ;—these were the indications of a spirit wounded by guilt, or sor- row, or perhaps both.

It was vain that her mother strove to restore her to health, or to raise her from dejection and despair. For a time, indeed, kindness and her native air seemed to check the ravages of cor- roding grief, and to delay the progress of that fatal disease which often bereaves the happy of a

sunny life, but which was in Susan the consequence of a broken heart. Medicine seemed but
to add new sufferings to the consuming fire which
wasted slowly, but unceasingly, the vigour of
her young frame. The minister of a religious
sect came; he spoke of condemnation to one
who refused to betray the cause of her anguish,
and the silent sorrows of the poor girl were
exchanged for delirium and paroxysms of mental agony. At last Mr. Bouverie visited her,
and to him eventually she imparted her story.
It is told in a few words. She had been led
astray by one who ought to have protected,
warned her, one who was virtually the guardian
of his young and ignorant inmates—in short,
by the gentleman in whose family she lived.
This individual taught her first to love him, and
she did really love him, for her's was no vulgar
mind,—and then took every advantage of that
unfortunate attachment, which the profligate
know so well how to take.

To the severe in judgment it may appear
some aggravation of his guilt that the person
whom he corrupted was one whom he had de-
puted to watch over the health, and safety, and

character of his young child!—that even with the innocent infant sleeping on her arm, he could dare to cherish an impure passion for her, whose image was associated in his mind with that of a father's dearest treasure. But the kind, indulgent, candid world judges not so harshly of an "indiscretion;" the poor victim is "base," "abominable," and must be dismissed, no matter whither; but "all men are alike, and they will do these things; and if it had not been known, it would not have signified." May God forgive them!

The affair was not discovered, but Susan "pined in thought." For a very short time only did she wrestle with her own conscience, and endeavour to reconcile herself with the thought that "others had done as she had." Consumption, arising from the united effects of a wounded conscience, and of a total indifference to the preservation of her own bodily health, soon made its appearance, and furnished for her a plea to leave the scene of her first and last sorrow—a sorrow which ceased only with her dying breath.

The man who virtually murdered her re-

mained prosperous, gay, and courted by a world
wilfully ignorant of the sins of the rich and the
agreeable. It is doubtful whether he would
even have remembered this one victim, had it
not been for a circumstance which occurred
after her death. When he accidentally heard
of that event, he sent poor Rose fifty pounds,
"from his sense of the services which Susan
had rendered to his child." It was returned
with disdain. " And tell him," said poor Rose,
as she got Mr. Bouverie to pen the few lines
which accompanied the returned gift, " that a
mother's curse should rest upon him, were it not
that *she* bade me to forgive him."

The expenses of the poor girl's last illness,
and of her funeral, were unostentatiously discharged by Mr. Bouverie; and that the bereaved mother might not feel that her child was
ignominiously laid among the nameless dead,
he placed a stone, with the simple inscription
before noticed, over her grave. He knew
also that the rustic monument would be a sort
of rallying point whereon the wretched survivor
might vent the sorrows of her heart: besides,
to ignorant, and consequently prejudiced minds,

a tombstone, however lowly, affords a tangible, and therefore consolatory memento of that which we have lost. We are comforted that one earthly fabric is still devoted to the departed object of fondness.

When Constance returned through the churchyard, after this conversation, she could not help pausing and ruminating some time upon the story, and wondering if the moral conveyed in the history of that simple tombstone would touch the heart of selfish and designing man. But she stopped not long, for Miss Monckton, who had promised to meet her on her return, now stepped forward to greet her.

" What shall you say," cried she, as they met, " if I have made an arrangement for you to go with me to Bath next week ? I have some very worthy friends there, to whom I wrote that, instead of my maid, I should bring with me, for a fortnight, a very ornamental young lady, of whose company I have grown fond, without knowing why or wherefore. I have already obtained the consent of your guardian, who thinks as highly of me as Solomon did of the Queen of Sheba. I give you no longer notice, because you can replenish your wardrobe much better at Bath than at Newberry."

" O, delightful! and how very kind of you!" said Constance.

" O, you know old maids have nothing else to do but to be kind, and the fancy I have taken for you is unaccountable; and yet, somehow or other, many people seem to have the same foible."

We pass over the adieux of Mr. and Mrs. Cattell, and even those of Mitten. Constance, as she quitted her sleeping-room, seemed to leave all dullness and care along with it. There was but one person whom she was sorry to leave, and that individual was Mr. Bouverie. She met him, the night before her departure, at one of the Newberry parties, at which his attendance had of late been very rare, and she was resolved to take leave of him, in a manner as cordial as her friendship for him dictated, and to seek every opportunity of speaking to him during the course of the evening. He appeared less to avoid her than formerly, and she was excited to more than her usual openness by this unexpected return to their former friendly converse.

" Do you know," said she to him, " how very kind Miss Monckton is to me? she is going to take me to Bath to-morrow."

" To Bath ?" exclaimed he, an air of deep vexation overclouding his countenance.

" Yes; and it is so very, very good of her; for whom have I to take me any where, or to give me any pleasure, but such friends as I may chance to obtain? And I am most grateful to any who feel an interest in me."

" There are many who must do so, Miss Courtenay," he said, in a low voice.

" Will you tell me—will you advise me," said Constance, encouraged by his soft and yet pensive manner, " what books to procure at Bath? I would rely on your judgment sooner far than that of any one whom I know; perhaps it will be too much trouble for you, to make me out a little list of such as you would recommend ?"

This was most persevering; yet Mr. Bouverie did not feel flattered by it. He was not, in this instance, particularly gratified by being treated only as the staid monitor and wise adviser, whilst all the warmth and interest were reserved for another.   For a few minutes, he made no reply.

"I shall be writing to Sir Charles Marchmont, and will take the liberty of enclosing a list of such books as may suit you."

"Sir Charles Marchmont! is he in Bath?" cried Constance, her colour mounting to her face and neck.

Mr. Bouverie's face was somewhat reddened also.   He answered her gravely, and almost, as she thought, reprovingly, "He has been there some time."

"But it is very likely that we may not see him," said she, "and therefore you had better send it direct to Miss Monckton, or to me."

"Whichever you please, Miss Courtenay; but you are sure to see Sir Charles, I think."

"Ah," thought Constance, "if I had suffered Mr. Bouverie to send me this list through him, I should have been sure to have seen him. Why was I so foolish? But why should I," again she reflected, "seek to draw forth the attentions of Sir Charles, or of any one? Am I not degrading myself in the very wish?"

" You are more serious and thoughtful, Miss Courtenay, than young ladies are wont to .be, when on the eve of expected enjoyment," said Mr. Bouverie, after a pause. " I hope that no misgivings as to the reality of the happiness which you anticipate, have crossed your mind."

Constance looked at him surprised. " You read my thoughts," she replied.

" God grant," said he, with earnestness, " that my misgivings concerning you may be visionary; that ——." He checked himself suddenly.

" Tell me what you fear for me," said Constance, eagerly.

" O, my fears are perhaps mere delusions of my own fancy," he answered, with a faint smile; " I can never anticipate that any real harm can happen to one so guileless and so candid as yourself."

" Besides, I have an excellent adviser in Miss Monckton ?" said Constance.

Mr. Bouverie was silent; he looked down, until Constance again urged her question.

" No one can appreciate more highly than I do," he answered, " Miss Monckton's excellent

qualities, both of the heart and of the head ; but she, too, may sometimes be deceived by appearances. Pardon me, I have perhaps said too much; you led to it yourself, by alluding to what you called your friendless condition. Friendless it can never be whilst you continue what you are," he added, his eyes resting upon her with an expression which, however grave, had somewhat of tenderness in it.

"You are afraid, I see," said Constance, playfully, "that I shall be corrupted by the vanities of the world at Bath."

"No; you have too much sensibility to be immoderately vain; vanity implies, or rather, perhaps, produces selfishness; that is its worst consequence. You feel too much for others to become selfish : it is not that I dread your becoming indifferent to the happiness of others; I tremble lest you should lose your own—but, indeed, I am wrong to say so much."

"What are you two talking so much about?" said the elder Miss Seagrave, her lack-lustre grey eyes acquiring the same sort of significancy as those of her domestic companion, the cat.

"They have been full twenty minutes in conversation." whispered Miss Pearson, to Mrs. Crawfurd.

" Miss Courtenay's such a very engrossing young lady," drawled out the latter, with a sweet smile.

" Miss Courtenay, I shall write a *billet doux* to Sir Charles, and tell him to look after you at Bath," said Mrs. De Courcy, her dark eyes brightening at the happiness of finding an excuse to mention his name ; " he must report progress of your flirtations to Mr. Bouverie."

" And of his own, to Mrs. De Courcy," said Miss Monckton.

" O you wicked creature, how you do quiz me about Sir Charles," cried Mrs. De Courcy, quite pleased, since she had not the reality, to have at least the credit of a flirtation with him.

" She had better run after him to Bath," said Miss Pearson, aside to Mrs. Crawfurd, " 'tis not so far as to London."

" Come, Miss Courtenay, make your adieux," said Miss Monckton to her, " for we must rise at six to-morrow.—Farewell, ladies ; good bye, Mrs. De Courcy, we shall bring Sir Charles back with us."

"O, Miss Monckton, how can that concern me?"

"Adieu, Miss Pearson, don't trouble yourself to get up in the morning to see how many
packages we have; I will tell you now—just
thirteen. Adieu, Mrs. Crawfurd, you are
always so amiable, that I am sure you will be
grieved to the soul if you hear we are over-
turned."

"I hope, indeed, you'll *not fall out* by the
way," said the placid widow, with a grim smile
at the wit of her double meaning.

"Miss Seagraves, I hope to see one and all
of you as blooming and cheerful as you are
now, when I come back," said Miss Monckton
to three very haggard looking old maids. "And
now, Mr. Bouverie, God bless you, and don't
be too apprehensive for Miss Courtenay and
me," said she, with a warm shake of the hand.
"We shall do very well, and return as heart-
whole, as we go—come, Constance."

"You will allow me to walk home with you,"
said Mr. Bouverie, hurriedly, for he dared
not trust himself before so many strangers, to
bid adieu to Miss Courtenay. Permission to

accompany them was readily granted. The darkness of the night concealed his agitation, as they proceeded down the quiet streets of the town, preceded by Mrs. Cattell's boy, holding a little lanthorn. It was necessary first to deposit Miss Monckton, and then Constance and Mr. Bouverie were left alone together. He took but little advantage of this circumstance, however, and scarcely spoke, until they reached Mr. Cattell's door, where pressing her hand fervently, he bade her farewell.

Mean time, the coterie which they had left assembled, continued together for a little while longer, in order to criticize the conduct of those from whom they had just parted.

" How strange Miss Monckton is !" said the elder Miss Seagrave, in a deep growling voice.

" And how she spoils that Miss Courtenay !" added the second, in a strong provincial accent.

" Miss Monckton having never been married, has no notion of the way in which young people should be managed," observed Mrs. Hemming, one of those ladies who are virtual representatives of the multiplication table, she having on an average, been blessed or afflicted with two children in three years, during the foregoing fifteen.

"I wonder how Miss Courtenay will look at Bath," said Mrs. De Courcy, wistfully.

"Oh, she'll be quite in the dolefuls," observed Miss Pearson, "without Mr. Bouverie."

"I'll lay my life that he follows her there," cried one of the Miss Seagraves, maliciously.

"There will be no occasion," replied Mrs. Crawfurd, with her angelic smile, "for she's sure to come back to *him*."

CHAPTER XVI.

A solemn, antique gentleman of rhyme,
Who having angled all his life for fame,
And getting but a nibble at a time,
Still fussily keeps fishing on, the same
Small "Triton of the minnows," the sublime
Of mediocrity, the furious same,
The echo's echo, usher of the school
Of female wits, boy bards.

BYRON.

In the course of the second day after their departure from Newberry, Constance and Miss Monckton found themselves in Bath. The former had been prepared by her friend to form some notion of the characters of the lady and gentleman whom she was going to visit. Accordingly, when she entered the drawing-room of Mr. and Mrs. Kilderby, she was not surprised, though there was no human being in the room, to find it tenanted; for four fine large white cats, with silver collars, ran out from under the sofa to greet them.

"These will be, in part, your companions," whispered Miss Monckton; "for Mrs. Kilderby can think and talk of nothing but her family. Allow me to introduce you—Miss Daphne, Miss Chloe, Mr. Apollo, and Mrs. Frisk."

A maid servant, neat to the last degree, with a curtsy such as Constance thought could hardly have been elucidated from a Bath servant, showed them to their several apartments; for Mrs. Kilderby was at her toilet, preparatory to dinner.

"Am I in Bath?" said Constance to herself; for, from the precise, papered-up, well-blinded, undisturbed look of the rooms through which she passed, she almost feared that she was going to her dull apartment at Mr. Cattell's again. But she soon found that she was in a very different atmosphere. Whatever Mrs. Kilderby might be, the genius of literature had visited her husband, and bestowed some of her gifts upon him; but she had bestowed such only as constituted the torment, rather than the glory of the poor good man; having given him the desire of distinction, without the power of obtaining it. If the itch of writing eternal epigrams without point, and impromptus without spirit, be poetic fire, Mr. Kilderby was a poet. If the practice of depositing on every lady's table some effusion of his brain—if labouring to get his name in the newspapers—scribbling vapid verses in the magazines—leaving bon-mots gratuitously in every grotto, arbour, summer-house, bathing-machine, on every inn window, remarkable stone, or prodigious tree, with the initials W. K. inscribed under each effort of his travelling muse,—if these and other exertions could have provoked public curiosity, and made a name, Mr. Kilderby would have been deemed by the time he arrived at his fiftieth year, little inferior to the voluminous Pope, or the indefatigable Dryden. But, by that time, his muse had become a public nuisance, defacing all common-place books, by covering good paper with bad verse. His acquaintances were as much alarmed when he talked of " Rhythm," as if he had proposed a duel; and one old gentleman who had borne his whims, for old acquaintance' sake, with great patience, was at

length heard to declare that he would rather
Mr. Kilderby would ask him to lend him a
thousand pounds, than bother him with one of
his impromptus. To close this digression, the
present aim of Mr. Kilderby was to get a pub-
lisher and puffer for a poem of his, in ten
cantos, written in imitation of the "New Bath
Guide," but as little to be compared in its execution to that successful production, as a delicately seasoned French dish is to a Scotch
haggis. Unhappily for the world, but most
unhappily for Constance, Lord Nelson had died
just before she paid her visit to Bath, and
Mr. Kilderby was "at him" for ever. No form
of Monody, Elegy, "Lines on a recent event,"
"Reflections on Trafalgar," were unemployed,
to vary, if possible, dull thoughts under new
aspects, and to disguise old ones with fresh
names.

Mrs. Kilderby was just the reverse of her
husband; her character was the antidote to his.
She was to him what the alkali in a saline
draught is to the acid. She was one of those
hard-headed women of the old school, who considered imagination and feeling as pernicious

weeds, to be exterminated, if possible, from
the fertile soil of the human mind. Her education had begun with working a sampler,
and had been considered finished when she
could master six columns of spelling at a
breath, and could play the "Fall of Paris"
without stopping. Reading, she deemed to be
the worst species of idleness, an expensive and
conceited sort of amusement. Wit, she con-
founded with profaneness, sentiment with licentiousness, and talent of all kinds, except for
cookery and needle-work, she regarded as impertinence. With all this, it was astonishing
what a nice sort of woman she really was. She
had a natural shrewdness, which had been much
improved by a long intercourse with the world,
and which her husband's follies had called into
play. She had a kind heart and a generous
disposition, but a bad temper; but this her
friend, Miss Monckton, was wont to excuse
on this head—that a certain portion of the
vixen in a woman's composition is to be accounted a sort of merit; it is the principle which keeps her servants in order, and
makes her friends look up to her. Accord-

ing to Miss Monckton, ill-tempered people
are always much better used than good-natured ones; every one gives way to them for
the sake of peace, and those who are inclined
to trample will always find a camomile plant
somewhere or other. It might have been al-
leged with more propriety, that Mrs. Kilderby
had much to irritate her, if seeing her husband
ridiculous, and knowing him to be a most
fitting representative of the word "bore," be
not enough to vex a woman who is not blessed
with forbearance. It is true that she had one
foible—a love for her cats; but this resulted in
a great measure both from her not having enjoyed the precarious blessing of children, and
from the utter departure of her affection from
that other natural channel, her husband; for
whilst her duty forbade her to hate, she
knew of no human or divine regulation which
prohibited her despising him.

Such were the couple with whom Miss
Monckton and her young friend were destined
to pass the period of their residence in Bath.
Mr. Kilderby had been catering about the
Pump-room for several days previous to their

arrival, for a suitable addition to their first
day's dinner circle; for as he always wished
particularly to shine in Miss Monckton's eyes,
he was anxious not only to enhance her pleasure, but to invite such persons as were likely
to impress her with a notion of his superior attainments. Next to his wife, he dreaded Miss
Monckton more than any one living; and this
dread was accompanied, not by dislike, for that
was too harsh a sentiment for his gentle nature
to cherish, but by a vast regard for her opinion,
and tenaciousness about her approbation.

Mr. Kilderby could succeed in bringing in
no other coadjutors to his weak party in his
own house, but Doctor Creamly, a young
physician recently established at Bath, a man
of acknowledged polite breeding, of sentiment not unvaried by wit; and of extensive
knowledge on every subject, except his profession. What Dr. Creamly wanted in medical skill, he made up for by his cleverness in
the art of pleasing. He adapted himself to
every person's temper and fancies—to the
grave, the gay, the loose, and the severe.
'Like' the vane on a church steeple, he veered

round to every point of the compass, and yet retained his own station and opinion.

" He has the highest views of human nature," whispered Mr. Kilderby to Miss Monckton; " the most elevated moral sentiments of any man I ever met with. He is all purity of mind and religious feeling."

" Hum," said Miss Monckton.

" Do you know, he says he thinks my little stanzas on Amanda equal to Goldsmith? Have you read them?"

" No."

" What! did I not send them to you? I thought I had. Then you shall have them," —in a tone of kind consideration.

" You are very good; but you have written me out so many of your things, that I cannot think of troubling you any more."

" I shall have the greatest pleasure in presenting you with a copy of it; and if you like to give it to Smith, the editor of the Newberry Advertiser, I shall have no objection."

" Indeed! that is too liberal," said Miss Monckton, her thin face without one smile of encouragement in it.

" Though he doesn't deserve it, for I sent him my ode on the king's recovery, and lines on Emma, and he never inserted either of them. It's all jealousy—pique—private pique. Don't you think so, Miss Courtenay?" for he ventured not to address this question to Miss Monckton.

" It is very unamiable, if it is," said Constance.

" Nothing," said Dr. Creamly, "can exceed the illiberality of the publishers of the daily press; they have no generosity of sentiment, no philosophical or extended views, no philanthropic desires for the moral improvement of our nature."

" They don't choose to put in things that don't answer, I suppose," said Mrs. Kilderby, sharply.

" True," said Dr. Creamly.

" They have behaved very ill to me," said Mr. Kilderby, emboldened by the presence of his aide-de-camp, Dr. Creamly, to venture upon the story of his wrongs.

" They have," said Dr. Creamly.

" How, pray?" said Constance, who felt inclined to take Mr. Kilderby's part among the Philistines, both domestic and foreign.

"It is a long story," said Mrs. Kilderby, her sharp hooked nose looking sharper than ever. "And pray, Mr. Kilderby, do let us entertain Miss Monckton and Miss Courtenay with something better than *that*."

There was a dead silence for a few minutes.

"How are the theatres attended now, Doctor Creamly?" said Miss Monckton.

"Very well, I believe," answered the physician, hesitatingly. "Very well, I believe."

"Theatres don't suit Dr. Creamly," said Mrs. Kilderby; "he's better away from them; might be sent for, you know."

"Of the stage, as a vehicle for moral sentiment, I think highly," said Dr. Creamly; "but I confess, the sock and buskin are so profaned by buffoonery and impropriety now, that I seldom go, unless it be to sigh over the recollection of Shakspeare, or to endeavour to recal the genius of Massinger."

"The dra-a-ma," said Mr. Kilderby, "is at a low ebb; don't you think so, Miss Courtenay? Ah, well a day! They rejected my poor

Clorintha ! and I declare if I don't think she would have made as good a figure as any of them ; don't you think so, Dr. Creamly ?"

The announcement of dinner waved the difficulty of an answer to this question. The snares which Mr. Kilderby was always laying to entrap the compliments of his friends were only, however, suspended. Constance felt truly sorry for him ; for much as she loved Miss Monckton, she pitied any one who came under her lash, especially when the whipcord of her satire was intertwined with the brambles of Mrs. Kilderby's temper.

" Poor Mr. Kilderby !" thought she. " At any rate, he has not a grovelling mind. He has a desire of fame, which might do credit to Burns or Cowper, and it is not his fault if Nature have given him the wish to rise, without the wings to fly."

But soon, she ceased to feel compassion for one whose vanity was a perpetual feast to him, and who was, therefore, no object of lamentation. The neatly served and well cooked dinner was scarcely disarranged by the devastations of the carving-knife, when a thundering knock at the door was heard. Mr. Kilderby, who was no great adept at carving, was working away upon a goose, his elbow lifted considerably above the altitude of his bald and shining head, and was meekly, but unprofitably enduring the instructions of his more skilful wife, when the servant announced—"Sir Charles Marchmont in the drawing room."

"Sir Charles who?" cried Mrs. Kilderby, "why does he call at this hour, Mr. Kilderby?" But Mr. Kilderby had vanished without waiting for the prohibition to move, which he expected.

"I didn't know that Mr. Kilderby was acquainted with Sir Charles Marchmont," said Miss Monckton to her hostess.

"Nor I either, Miss Monckton; but he's always picking up some one or other at the pump-room. Lord! what makes the man call at this hour? why it's four o'clock. Well, there he's gone now, I hear the door shut. Miss Courtenay wants her dinner—she looks pale, I think."

"She looked red enough just now," thought Miss Monckton; "I see how it is, in spite of all her bravery. Well, Mr. Kilderby, and how is my friend Sir Charles?"

"Remarkably charming! He's a fine creature," returned Mr. Kilderby, with a smile, denoting extreme self-satisfaction. "Do you know, Mrs. K., that as I was standing with Captain Perry to-day, Sir Charles Marchmont, hearing that I was the author of Clorintha, a Tragedy, and other Poems"——

"Come now, Mr. Kilderby, do get on with that goose."

"Says I to Captain Perry—a wing, Miss Courtenay? Come, now, if the wing had a quill in it, it would be no bad thing—a poet's gray goose-quill, you know."

"Mr. Kilderby, help me to a slice off the breast," screamed his wife, her small dark eyes glistening with inspiration, but not of a poetical kind.

"You were telling us about Sir Charles Marchmont," said Miss Monckton. Mr. Kilderby again laid down his knife and fork.

"Do you know, Miss Monckton—do you know, I find it absolutely inconvenient and overpowering to go to the rooms. The number

of people that ask to be introduced to one at
Bath, so glad, you know, to catch hold of a
literary person, a bit of a poet, like me—only
a bit of a one "—looking at Dr. Creamly to be
contradicted; but Dr. Creamly was under the
shadow of Mrs. Kilderby's presence, and dared
not lend his assistance at this juncture.

"I never heard that Sir Charles was particularly of a literary turn, did you?" said Miss
Monckton, appealing to Constance.

"I never heard—I am no judge," replied
the latter.

"Pardon me, but I think you have a sweet
taste," said Mr. Kilderby, "and I shall see
how you like my sonnet to a Blue Bell, after
dinner."

"I thought you had put that in the fire long
ago, Mr. Kilderby," said his wife.

"And as I was saying to Sir Charles, I
understood from my clever friend here, Miss
Monckton, that you were highly accomplished."

"How came you to speak of her? Tell us
the whole history of your meeting with Sir
Charles," cried Miss Monckton, upon whom a
new light now broke.

" Why, as I was saying, Sir Charles, I know, knew me to be the author of Clorintha, and was eyeing me all over; but that we literary men are used to, you know, at Bath, Dr. Creamly."

" Everywhere, everywhere, sir, society rallies around talent."

" Mr. Kilderby, do send away that goose," cried Mrs. Kilderby,—and the goose was at length dismissed.

" He has left one of his flock behind him," thought Miss Monckton.

" Alas!" said Constance to herself, " shall we never come back to Sir Charles?"

" Literature," pursued Dr. Creamly, by way of fill up, " is to our intellectual system, what air is to our animal system—it refines and elevates mankind. I am, myself, of opinion, that knowledge, widely diffused, will bring about, by slow and sure degrees, that universal benevolence and moral elevation, which alone can approximate us to perfection. What do you think, my dear madam," said he to Mrs. Kilderby, " of the moral perfectibility of our nature?"

" I think nothing of it at all," was her reply.

" How exalted Dr. Creamly's sentiments are!" whispered Mr. Kilderby to Miss Courtenay. " What a fine mind he has !"

" Well, and were Sir Charles's glances at you followed by no explicit declaration of his admiration of the author of Clorintha ?" asked Miss Monckton.

" I assure you I felt much flattered, my good friend, to find my poor productions so much taken up by the higher classes; for I am told Sir Charles is a man of the first fashion and connexions here.—But I'll tell you all about it, if my good Mrs. Kilderby will let me."

" O you'll tell it, whether or no, Mr. Kilderby, some time or another, so we had better have it all out now."

" I had been asking my friend Perry to dine with us to-day—he trafficks with the Muses like myself, a little—says I to him, ' We are to have Hebe and Minerva to dine with us to-day.' ' Nonsense,' says he, ' it's some of your freaks of fancy ;'—' But we are,' replied I, ' two very charming ladies from ——shire; one—excuse me, Miss Monckton—has been younger; the

other, they tell me, is divine as a poet's dream,'
bowing to Miss Courtenay.—'And what's her
name?' says the Captain—now excuse me,
Miss Courtenay, if I couldn't at first remember
it—my poor head, as Mrs. Kilderby says, is
full of Florimels, and Chloe's, and such like—I
can't just tell her name, but she's young, I'm
told, and beautiful as my own Clorintha, and
she lives at Newberry. 'Sir Charles,' says
Perry, turning round to the young Baronet
who was at a little distance, 'you know Newberry, can you furnish my good friend here
with a name?' Now when he had told him
that you were brought here, Miss Courtenay, by
Miss Monckton ; and more particularly when
I added that you might have been, I was told,
an original for my Clorintha, (a very great compliment, let me tell you,) he said he had no
doubt but that it was Miss Courtenay—but
what he added, I must not tell you, I suppose, or your good duenna there will be angry
with me."

" Please to finish your story, Mr. Kilderby,"
said his wife; "James is waiting for the
pigeons—don't you see?"

"And then, Miss Monckton, Captain Perry was commissioned soon afterwards, by Sir Charles, to introduce him to me. I think it a singular compliment; for though I have often been in Sir Charles's company before, he has never made the request. I attribute it entirely to my Clorintha."

"Or to her resemblance," said Dr. Creamly, in his sweetest tone.

But his host was too much elated to be astonished at this insinuation from his aide-de-camp. He even let out a secret, which he would not have dared to disclose except before company, to Mrs Kilderby, namely, that he had asked Sir Charles to dinner. "He called, however," added the poet, "with many excuses, to say that he was obliged to dine at Lord Somebody's, Lord Vallefort's, I think; but that if I would let him call in the evening, he should be happy to be introduced to Mrs. Kilderby, and to see his Newberry friends; so he'll look in upon you, Mrs. K., my dear, between eight and nine."

"He'll not look much at me, Mr. Kilderby, I dare say."

" Constance must be blind, if she does not see through all this," thought Miss Monckton; "for it is obvious to me, that all this sudden solicitude to be introduced, had a very different source, than anxiety to see the author of Clorintha: but let that pass."

" Doctor," cried Mr. Kilderby, who was in great good humour, as they entered the drawing room, " I mean to introduce you especially to Sir Charles, for no doubt he may be a great friend to you in your professional advancement, and a word from me may do wonders, you know. That is the advantage of having a little fame oneself," said he, looking at Miss Courtenay for her support to this opinion.

" O, I am sure you are very kind—very kind," said Dr. Creamly, without raising his dark eyes from the ground, where they were usually directed; "but I am the worst person in the world to look after my professional advancement, and to seek new friends and fresh acquaintance. I absolutely shrink from the thought of encountering a new patient."

" Humph," said Miss Monckton, " that's uncommon."

"And it's lucky that all doctors are not of the same way of thinking, otherwise we should never be able to change our physician," said Mrs. Kilderby sharply.

"And I am sure," said Constance, "I should be very sorry if I were obliged always to have the attendance of Dr. Stately when I am ill. He prescribed for me, when I had a cough last winter, and he used so many technical terms, and talked so much *secundum artem*, that if I had a dictionary of medical phrases at hand, I should have enlightened myself, if possible—as it was——"

But the conclusion of her speech was interrupted by the entrance of Sir Charles Marchmont. It was now four months since Constance had seen him, and she felt it but too probable, that a total change of sentiment towards her had taken place, since the happy delusive days of their autumnal walks through scenes enhanced in beauty, as Moore expresses it, by "seeing them reflected in looks that we love." She deemed it also likely, that the temporary irritation in Sir Charles's mind towards her, had also passed away with the interest which had perhaps partly occasioned it: with respect to his engagement with Miss Herbert, she had become of late incredulous, partly from the positive assertions of Miss Monckton, and partly from her confidence in Sir Charles's honour and single-heartedness, which would, she ignorantly trusted, have prevented his paying to any woman the close attentions which he had devoted to her, whilst his hand was affianced to another. Impressed with these considerations, she had prepared herself to receive him as an acquaintance, but resolved promptly, not perhaps firmly, that she would never again renew the intimacy of former days, an intimacy which had caused her so much pain, had evidently been forgotten by him, and which she dared not trust her own-heart again to permit. Sir Charles thought himself obliged to make the whole circuit of the company before he spoke to Miss Courtenay, and when he did, she rose, (it was then the custom for ladies to rise,) and received him with a modest cordiality of manner, which few well informed men will misunderstand, or mistake for encouragement.

She had now the advantage of Sir Charles, for, though much accustomed to conceal his feelings, he could not, for some moments, recover his composure after speaking to her.

To the disappointment of Mr. Kilderby, the conversation turned entirely on general subjects, of which literature formed but a small portion; and with all his efforts, he could only quote one stanza of his lines upon Emma, and get in a stave from Clorintha once. Sir Charles had first a great deal to ask about Newberry, but it was observable that he addressed his inquiries chiefly to Miss Monckton, although Constance joined readily and artlessly in the conversation. Constance was therefore left chiefly to converse with Dr. Creamly, who, with the manners of a saint, had a considerable portion of worldly discernment, where beauty, influence, or riches were to be found, and conciliated. Mrs. Kilderby sat on her hard sofa, fretting and watching her feline family, or, as they were called by the household, the " young ladies," and alternately stirring the fire herself, or scolding Mr. Kilderby for meddling with it;

whilst her good man fidgetted about the room, began anecdotes about himself to Miss Monckton and Sir Charles, or looked into those papers and magazines from which he could elicit a little praise to himself.

" His literature," whispered Sir Charles to Miss Monckton, " is all of the Kilderberian school; and I fancy he quotes no poetry but what is of the Kilderberian stanza."

" Miss Courtenay, Sir Charles is not at all reformed since he was at Newberry," said Miss Monckton.

" I am very sorry for it; I thought it would be otherwise."

" Did you expect to find me changed ?" said Sir Charles, in a low tone, and with a manner not to be misunderstood ; " if so, you are mistaken."

Constance determined to be, or if she could not be, to seem insensible to this renewal of old ways. " I have bartered indifference for anxiety once," said she, to herself; " but it shall be so no more." She tried to fix her attention to what Dr. Creamly was saying to her, but found herself, despite her wishes, perpetually listening to what Miss Monckton and Sir Charles

were talking about, opposite to her. Once or
twice she happened to look across when Sir
Charles's eyes were directed full on her, with
an expression so full of melancholy, so different
to his usually sparkling glances, that she was
softened, notwithstanding all her resolutions.
Yet her natural sense of what was due to herself, still deterred her from showing her partiality to a man, who, whilst he evidently wished her to believe him attached to her, forbore
from explicitly avowing his own sentiments.
Miss Monckton saw with regret the manifest
resolution made by her young friend to see, as
if she saw it not, the obvious attachment of Sir
Charles to her.

"He already suspects her of a preference
to Bouverie," thought the good old maid, "and
this will confirm his suspicions. I am satisfied
that Sir Charles will never make an offer, without being sure of its acceptance. And yet,
how admirably they are suited to each other!
How will her mind, and manners, and person,
and heart, grace his station, and again raise the
name of Lady Marchmont to honour! And
how will his warm, but thoughtless heart be

devoted to her, and his character thus rescued from the dissipation but too incident to
his station. I must see what I can do."

Thus reasoning, and with the best intentions
possible, Miss Monckton meditated a course of
proceedings as mischievous, and finally as fatal
to the happiness of those whom she sought to
serve, as the manœuvres of those who seek to
interfere with Heaven's decrees usually are.
Since marriages are, by proverbial consent,
made above, it is dangerous for mortals below
to meddle with them.

" Sir Charles," said Mr. Kilderby, as the
young Baronet was taking leave, "allow me
particularly to recommend to your notice during your stay in Bath, my friend, Dr. Creamly,
whose only fault is his too great opinion of me.
You'll find him a man of a thousand. And if,"
in an audible whisper, " you can introduce him
to Lord Vallefort, so much the better."

" My uncle leaves Bath to-morrow, or I
should have been most happy," said Sir Charles.

" How strange," thought Constance, "that he
should hurry away from Miss Herbert the last
night, if things be true."

" Then I presume you will be going away soon, Sir Charles?" asked Miss Monckton.

" Not immediately; it is too great a pleasure for me to see so old a friend as you are, to run away from you immediately. I want to assist Mr. Kilderby in showing you some of the lions of Bath."

" He has begun by showing you himself," said Mrs. Kilderby, as she sat squeezed up in her corner, her face puckered up with crossness and fatigue, and scarcely any of her features legible but her eyes.

" Then I shall venture to call about twelve to-morrow, may I, Miss Monckton?"

" You may—but you must take your chance of finding us in good or bad humour; we may be inclined to walk, we may be determined to stay at home."

" I shall abide in *hope*," said Sir Charles, " for it is my nature to hope, despite fate and fortune."

" It is the nature of all of you," said Mrs. Kilderby, " where your own personal vanity is concerned."

" Talking of hope," said her consort, " did

you ever happen to notice, Sir Charles, four lines of mine on that subject, in my verses on the Seasons, published in the European Magazine?"

"I have not happened to meet with them," said Sir Charles, who was just at the.door.

"Indeed! I am surprised, for they were in every body's mouth. You have, Dr. Creamly."

Dr. Creamly was obliged to confess that he had not; "he never read the European."

"And never read the poetry in it, I dare say," said Mrs. Kilderby, her eyes glaring like one of her own cats.

"I should think that Dr. Creamly's studies lay chiefly in Galen and the Pharmacopœia," remarked Miss Monckton, who, like many other ladies, had an illiberal prejudice against medical men who cultivated any thing but their own art.

"My studies are few, and not worthy of observation," replied the Doctor, with an air of profound modesty.

"He studies from nature, perhaps," said Mrs. Kilderby, with an arch look at Miss Courtenay.

The Doctor smiled and bowed, and looked
ineffably overcome by the notice which he had
excited; and thus the evening closed.

END OF VOL. I.

LONDON:

IBOTSON AND PALMER, PRINTERS, SAVOY STREET, STRAND.